AMORE ITALIANO DUET

CARA MARSI

THE PAINTED LADY PRESS

Published by The Painted Lady Press United States of America

First Electronic Edition: May 2019
Second Electronic Edition: October 2020

This book is a work of Fiction and all characters exist solely in the author's imagination. Any resemblance to persons, living or dead, is purely coincidental. Any references to places, events or locales are used in a fictitious manner.

Cover by Harris Channing

Formatting by Aileen Fish

Cover copy created by BlurbWriter.com

ISBN: 978-0-9969811-4-9

AUTHOR'S NOTE

On our last trip to Italy, my husband and I spent a wonderful day exploring the Medieval city of Ravello, on Italy's Amalfi Coast. I fell in love with the magic of Ravello, the narrow, winding streets, the ancient buildings, and the majestic views of the Mediterranean. I knew I had to write a story set there. I hope I've done the city justice.

CURATING LOVE

AMORE ITALIANO 1

Cara Marsi

Published by The Painted Lady Press United States of America

First Electronic Edition: May 2019

Second Electronic Edition: October 2020

Cover by Harris Channing

Formatting by Aileen Fish

Cover copy created by BlurbWriter.com

All the color drained out of Chloe Decker's world when her fiancé died. But now her new Master of Fine Arts degree and a letter inviting her to curate the art collection of the wealthy and prominent DiMarco family of Ravello, Italy, lets Chloe begin to picture a new life for herself. This temporary job will be a great stepping stone to her ultimate goal of opening her own art gallery in her hometown of Philadelphia. But she'd never imagined including the sexy grandson of her employer in that portrait.

Matteo DiMarco, the playboy scion of the DiMarco family, will never again let a woman betray him. Casually dating some of the world's most beautiful women works for him and keeps him from losing his heart again. But sweet, beautiful, earthy Chloe reawakens old dreams of a life more fully lived.

Wary of losing her heart again, Chloe's not ready for a relationship, not even with a fine Italian masterpiece of a man like Matteo. Besides, her future is in Philadelphia, not Italy. Can Matteo convince her to stay and take a chance on him? Can she open her heart and paint a new picture that includes them both?

CHAPTER 1

University of Pennsylvania
School of Arts and Sciences
Philadelphia, PA

Ms. Chloe Decker
Philadelphia, PA

Dear Ms. Decker,

Congratulations on earning your Master of Fine Arts degree from the University of Pennsylvania. We are pleased to inform you that you have been chosen by the DiMarco family of Ravello, Italy, and the faculty of the School of Arts and Sciences for the position of curator of the extensive Sofia DiMarco art collection.

Competition for this coveted job was fierce. Due to your high grades and broad knowledge of all disciplines of art, we feel you are well-qualified for this sought-after position.

We estimate this to be a two-to-three-month assignment. Room and board will be provided at the DiMarco villa in Ravello, along with a small stipend.

Please contact our office as soon as possible to make travel arrangements.

Our best to you in your future endeavors.

Sincerely,

John Randall, Dean
University of Pennsylvania
School of Arts and Sciences

* * *

Ravello, Italy

"Q*uanto*? How much?" Chloe Decker rubbed her finger over the etched flower motif on the silver pendant attached to a heavy silver chain. She looked expectantly at the merchant selling his wares at a vendor stand in Ravello's Duomo Square. The sun-filled square, colorful and crowded with tourists and natives enjoying the warm June day, hummed with activity.

The middle-aged merchant smiled, showing uneven teeth. "One hundred fifty dollars," he said in English.

Chloe frowned. She loved the pendant, but did she love it one hundred fifty dollars' worth? She'd been in Ravello a week now, working ten-hour days with the assistant hired by the DiMarco family cataloging their art collection. On this Saturday, her first day off, she intended to enjoy every minute until the DiMarco chauffeur came to drive her back to the villa in two hours.

As she pulled her wallet from her cross-body purse, a man's deep voice, speaking Italian, and very close to her, stopped her.

She raised her gaze to golden brown eyes framed by thick black lashes. She scanned the stranger slowly, savoring his stunning good looks. With chiseled features, sharp cheekbones, and narrow high-bridged nose, he could be a sculpture of Adonis, come to life to mingle with mere mortals. Thick black hair curled over the collar of his white dress shirt, and his rolled-up sleeves exposed muscular arms with a smattering of dark hair. Indigo jeans showcased long legs that seemed to go on forever. Tall for an Italian, he towered over her by a foot.

When her gaze traveled back to his face, his teasing grin told her he knew she checked him out and he liked it. She glanced quickly away.

The Adonis spoke something in rapid Italian to the merchant.

"*Mi dipiace, Signore DiMarco*," the merchant said. Chloe expected him to bow and scrape in front of the younger man.

Wait. Did the merchant call him "DiMarco?" The hot guy couldn't be related to the powerful DiMarcos of Ravello, her employers.

The merchant looked at her. "So sorry, *signorina*. I was mistaken about the price. It is seventy-five dollars."

"That sounds better." She took bills out of her wallet and paid him. He wrapped the necklace in tissue, placed it in a velvet bag, and handed it to her.

She stuffed the bag into her purse and turned her attention to the handsome Italian who'd helped her. Hoping he spoke English, she said, "I don't know what you said to him, but thank you."

"It is nothing," he said in perfect English with a lilting accent. "These merchants like to cheat the tourists. They give Ravello a bad name." He smiled, his teeth white against his olive skin. "The sellers expect you to bargain with them. Never pay the first price they give."

She returned his smile. "I'll remember that."

Interest sparked in his amazing eyes as he studied her. "You are American."

She held out her hand to shake his. "Chloe Decker."

Surprise flashed across his features. He took her hand and raised it to his lips to plant a light kiss on her knuckles. A thrill raced up her spine. Ohh! She could get used to hot guys kissing her hand. A sudden surge of anxiety squeezed her chest, making her excitement dissipate into the humid air. With schoolwork and grieving over Rob's death, she hadn't been attracted to another man in a very long time. She wouldn't start now, especially with a smokin' guy who probably had women falling all over him.

Releasing her hand, he said, "I am Matteo DiMarco. You are the American my grandfather hired to curate my grandmother's art collection?"

Chloe swallowed. He was one of *the* DiMarcos after all. "Yes, I am." Further words failed her and she could only stare as a collage of pictures formed in her mind. She'd studied the family before coming here. Matteo DiMarco, playboy scion of the wealthy and influential family, stood before her. In every photo of him she'd seen, he had a beautiful woman on his arm. She should have recognized him immediately, but in person, he radiated a vibrancy and sex appeal no picture could contain.

"My grandfather's words describing your loveliness don't do you justice," he said.

A charmer for sure. So not what she needed. She smiled politely against the flush of pleasure his words incited.

"It's good to finally meet you, Signorina Decker," he continued. "I've been away on business this last week. Now that I'm back, we'll see more of each other."

See more of him? She'd have to steel herself against his allure. She'd come to Italy for her career, not a fling with a playboy. "Call me Chloe, please, Signore DiMarco," she said in her best professional voice.

"And you must call me Matteo." He shot her another of his bone-melting smiles. "Signore DiMarco is my grandfather."

They moved away from the vendor stand. Someone in the crowd jostled her. Matteo grabbed her elbow to steady her. His touch sent a jolt of heat rocketing through her before she pulled away.

"I'll buy you lunch," he said. "It will be my welcome to our beautiful city."

"That's very nice of you, but I have more shopping to do. And Nunzio is picking me up in less than two hours."

Matteo pulled a phone from the pocket of his shirt. "I'll call our chauffeur and tell him I will drive you back. Then we'll have lunch."

His family employed her. Matteo only offered to buy her lunch and drive her back to the DiMarco palazzo. Not a big deal. "Okay."

CHAPTER 2

Three hours later, Matteo and Chloe walked through Ravello heading for his car parked outside the main square. He glanced down at her. His initial shock at finding the beautiful American worked for his grandfather had given way to a sweet pleasure he seldom knew these days.

Something about Chloe, with her large gray eyes, chin-length straight brown hair shot with gold highlights, and her trusting smile spoke to a piece of his heart that still believed in love, in life, the part Ingrid's betrayal had almost destroyed.

Bored with the models and actresses who needed the publicity of being seen with a DiMarco, he'd grown accustomed to going through life without actually feeling.

Chloe's excitement and enthusiasm as they'd toured Ravello helped him appreciate anew the beauty and pulse of the place where he'd grown up. She smiled brightly at the people they passed and at the merchants whose shops they entered. Others responded to her with smiles and nods and greetings in Italian and English. Seemed he wasn't the only one captivated by Chloe's appeal and friendliness. Her rapt attention when he regaled her with stories of his city's rich history made him swell with patriotic pride.

The vulnerability he sensed in Chloe's expressive eyes and around her wide mouth compelled him to want to know her better. Her full lips, pink and soft, begged him to kiss her. Like a rare flower, delicate and gentle, she needed special care.

When they got to his Maserati, he unlocked the car and walked around to the passenger side to open the door for her. As he gestured for her to get in, fear tightened her exquisite features and she hesitated.

"What's wrong, Chloe?"

"We're riding in that? Over those narrow, winding roads."

"Of course. It's my car."

"A fast car. Nunzio drove very slowly."

"I'm not an old man like Nunzio. I drive fast, and I'm careful. You'll be safe."

She glanced around, and he wondered if she considered bolting. Finally, she slid into the passenger seat and fastened her seat belt.

He got in the driver's side, clicked on his seat belt, and started the car. The engine roared to life, purring like a contented cat. He eased out of the parking spot and headed toward the Amalfi Coast and the short drive to the DiMarco palazzo.

He loved driving the hairpin turns along the coast, with the Mediterranean sparkling far below, a sea monster waiting to devour any cars unfortunate enough to fall over the steep cliffs. Driving relaxed him and made him feel alive, free of the constraints of his carefully cultivated public persona.

As he negotiated one particularly narrow turn, Chloe gasped beside him. He stole a quick glance at her and saw that her hands were clasped tightly on her lap. "It's okay, Chloe. You're safe."

"Please drive slower." Her voice came out thin and high.

He lowered his speed. The car behind him honked its horn and tailgated him even closer than he'd done before. Matteo shrugged. "You're afraid?" he asked her.

"Very. A—a close friend died three years ago in a horrific crash."

"I'm sorry, Chloe."

When they got to the villa, Chloe went to her room in the guest wing of the sprawling estate, and Matteo went in search of his grandfather. He found the elderly man on one of the patios enjoying a glass of wine.

"Grandfather." Matteo placed a hand on the old man's shoulder and bent to kiss his cheek before taking a seat across from him and pouring himself some wine.

His grandfather nodded and sipped his drink. "Did you have a good trip from Rome?"

"It was uneventful. I stopped off at Ravello as you asked and picked up your watch from the jewelry shop."

His grandfather's eyes twinkled. "Meet anyone interesting there?"

"I know you're capable of many things, Grandfather. Surely, you couldn't have known I'd meet Miss Decker."

Matteo narrowed his eyes. "What are you up to, you crafty old man?"

Matteo and his grandfather shared a special bond. Giuseppe DiMarco raised Matteo after Matteo's father, Domenico, died in a skiing accident when Matteo was five. Matteo's mother, Valentina, an international socialite, barely had time for her young son.

His grandfather laughed. "You give me too much credit. When Nunzio told me he would drive Miss Decker to Ravello today, I'd hoped if I put you there too, you'd meet her. I knew you'd notice a beautiful woman." Giuseppe sat back, looking as contented as a cat that had swallowed some cream. "What do you think of her?"

"She's beautiful in that innocent way American women have. And she's intelligent." Matteo waved a hand. "I have enough women in my life now."

"Bah! Those women are not good for you, my son."

"Being seen with beautiful models and actresses is good for business, ours and theirs. The subscriptions to our entertainment magazine go up every time we publish pictures of me with famous beauties. You know these women mean nothing to me other than as friends, and sometimes not even that."

"You should settle down," Giuseppe said. "Find a smart, talented young woman like Chloe Decker."

"Don't play matchmaker. I resist Mama when she tries. Much as I love you, stay out of my love life."

Matteo sipped his wine as a gentle breeze, tinged with the sweet scent of the flowers that grew in profusion over the low stone patio wall and down the path to the sea, ruffled his hair.

"You are almost thirty-three," his grandfather said, drawing his attention. "When I was your age, I had two sons and ran the DiMarco companies."

Matteo leaned closer and looked into his grandfather's light brown eyes, so like his own. "I don't plan to marry. I'm happy with my life as it is."

His grandfather's eyes softened. "Ingrid happened a long time ago. She is no good. Your uncle is welcome to her. You deserve better, but you must move on." The older man studied him. "Chloe Decker has a good soul. She is not like Ingrid and the others. You would do well with a woman like her."

Matteo held up a hand. "No more, Grandfather. I will live my own life."

CHAPTER 3

Dusky twilight splattered the Mediterranean sky with shades of pink, blue, and orange, reminding Chloe of a Jackson Pollock painting. With a contented sigh, she settled into her chair at the patio table and sipped the crisp white wine that had come from one of the DiMarco wineries, according to Anna, the maid who'd brought the wine. She'd also informed Chloe that Giuseppe DiMarco would not be joining her for dinner tonight, as he did most nights. Chloe would miss the company of the older man who treated her with kindness and respect, more like a member of the family than hired help. Since Anna hadn't mentioned Matteo, Chloe assumed he'd be having dinner elsewhere. She hadn't seen him since this afternoon when they'd driven back from Ravello.

She heard footsteps and turned to see Matteo step onto the patio. Their gazes connected, and something hot pulsed between them. She tossed back the last of her wine, as if she could drown out her attraction to Matteo.

"*Buonasera*, Chloe," Matteo said in his rich, deep voice that warmed her like fine aged wine.

"Hi, Matteo. Good evening to you, too." The calmness in her voice surprised her. She felt anything but calm.

He sat and poured himself a glass of wine. Anna, followed by other servants, appeared with platters of food.

Matteo's easy-going company and several glasses of wine helped Chloe relax during the scrumptious meal of Fettucine Alfredo served with escarole and tomatoes from the extensive DiMarco gardens. They topped off the meal with homemade vanilla gelato. During the leisurely dinner, she and Matteo talked about Italy, art, and Ravello. Smart, and knowledgeable about art, Matteo revealed nothing of the playboy she'd expected.

Nursing a demitasse cup of espresso, Chloe leaned back in her chair. "The food here is astounding. I'm going to weigh a ton when I get home."

His intense eyes scanned her. "A few pounds will not diminish your beauty."

Heat started at her neck and spread to her face. She knew she blushed, and hoped he didn't notice in the dim light from the candles set on the table. "Thank you. Much as I appreciate the compliments, I don't need them."

"Every woman should be told she is beautiful."

"Not all the time."

He jerked his head back, then barked out a laugh. His teasing gaze met hers again. "I never hand out empty compliments, Signorina. Your honesty is refreshing." He leaned closer. "You're beautiful and sweet, a most appealing combination."

She couldn't help laughing. "Okay. Enough." She held up her hands.

"Agreed. Enough compliments. For now. Have you seen our gardens yet?"

"Federico took me on a quick tour the day I arrived," she said, naming the DiMarco butler. "I've been working long hours and haven't had a chance to explore them again."

"You must see them in the moonlight." He stood and reached out a hand to her.

A moonlight walk with Matteo? Part of her prepared to run from his appeal. Another part of her reminded Chloe she was a big girl and could handle him and the excitement he provoked in her. "A walk sounds great."

CHAPTER 4

Matteo cupped her elbow, helping her negotiate the steep marble steps leading from the patio to the grounds. The moon left a sparkling path on the sea below and painted a picture of romance that made anticipation flow through Chloe. Night insects sang their tuneful songs and seemed to say, *Enjoy this night and this man. It's only temporary.*

She looked up into Matteo's eyes, shadowed in the semi-darkness. "Your palazzo and grounds are beautiful. You are very lucky."

He shrugged in the way Italians had perfected. "It's home."

As they strolled along the starlit cobblestone path, flowering shrubs, like silent sentinels, brushed them on both sides. Chloe inhaled the calming scents of thousands of flowers. The past three years had been a tightrope of grief interwoven with hard work. Maybe the time had finally come for her to put aside the heartbreak and sculpt a new life.

The pale light, the flowers swaying in the breeze, the cacophony of night sounds, and the vibrant man walking next to her, who dared her to dream again, wrapped Chloe in an enchanted world she'd never before known.

"Let's sit and enjoy the night." Matteo nodded toward a stone bench next to a marble sculpture that looked from the Ancient Roman era.

Chloe approached the statue and ran her hand over the pitted marble of the Roman god Bacchus holding up a goblet of wine. "Bacchus. This looks authentically ancient."

"It is."

Widening her eyes, she faced him. "You've got an Ancient Roman statue in your garden? I didn't think any of these were outside museums."

"When you're a DiMarco, you can have anything you want. Almost anything." His voice had taken on a hard quality and she wondered what things he wanted but couldn't have.

She sat on the bench and he joined her, sitting so close she felt the heat of his body. Not trusting herself too near the enticing Matteo, she moved slightly away.

"Are you afraid of me, Signorina Chloe Decker?"

She bristled. "Of course not."

"Don't worry. Despite what you read about me in the tabloids, I can be a gentleman."

Tempted to tell him she didn't want him to be a gentleman, she said instead, "You seem to date some of the world's most beautiful women."

"Not every picture tells the true story," he said softly. "You're more intriguing than any of those women."

"Me? Intriguing?"

"You're a beautiful woman who's not afraid to speak her mind. I don't often come across a woman like you."

"Maybe you've been looking in the wrong places."

He laughed, the sound appealing and seductive. "Maybe so."

The gentle lap of the sea lulled her into relaxing. The night settled around them. Above, the stars spread like diamonds on a black velvet sky. Chloe snuck a peek at Matteo. Her old life seemed very far away.

She sighed.

"Chloe." Matteo's whispered word caressed her.

She turned to find him staring at her, his eyes dark and mysterious in the moonlight.

He brushed his knuckles over her face, the gesture more sensual than any words. Grasping her shoulders, he pulled her gently to him.

When he bent to take her lips in a butterfly-soft kiss, she melted against him. She should resist. She didn't want to. Since the moment she'd seen him at Duomo Square, she'd wanted to taste him, to feel his full lips, to touch his chiseled face.

His lips firmed over hers, coaxing and teasing, urging her to give more. When he cupped her jaw, heat, like lava from nearby Mt. Vesuvius, scorched her. With a low groan, she wrapped her arms around his neck and gave herself over to the delicious feel of Matteo's lips and hands.

The squawk of a night bird broke the magical spell that held her in its grip. She pushed away from Matteo. Embarrassment and anxiety punched her like twin jabs to her solar plexus. She stood. "I need to get back."

As she turned to walk away, he stood and touched her arm until she faced him.

"I won't apologize," he said. "I've wanted to kiss you from the minute I laid eyes on you."

"I'm sure you say that to all the women." Confusion and shame made her blurt the harsh words. She headed back to the palazzo and the security of her room.

* * *

NURSING A TUMBLER OF WHISKEY, Matteo sat in the study. The quiet of the house seemed to mock him with the loneliness that had become his constant companion. The small lamp set on the eighteenth-century table next to the leather sofa cast shadows over the books lining the shelves, silent voyeurs to his muddled thoughts.

He shouldn't have taken liberties with Chloe. He knew better than to come on so strongly to a trusting woman like her. She was different from the hard-edged, sophisticated women he knew. From the first moment he'd seen Chloe, he'd wanted to kiss her full pink lips, to taste her sweetness. Not even Ingrid had affected him on first glance like Chloe. He'd had his share of involvements, and he knew how to protect his heart. This American woman with her earthy appeal had touched his soul and made him want to live fully again.

He wanted Chloe.

CHAPTER 5

"Let's take a break," Chloe said to her assistant Francesca, an art student, at ten the next morning. They'd been working since eight in the building constructed on the sprawling DiMarco property to house and show the collection.

Despite how busy they'd been, Chloe's mind kept drifting to Matteo and the kiss they'd shared last night. His lips seemed imprinted on hers. Thinking about him and that hot kiss warmed her more than the sunlight slanting through the large Palladian windows.

Rubbing her lower back, Chloe stood from her crouched position where she'd been sorting through framed paintings. Blinking to relax her eyes, she focused on her surroundings. With pale hardwood floors, white walls, and numerous windows plus skylights, the one-story modern building presented a good frame in which to showcase the art. Two offices and a small employee break room, complete with a top-of-the line Italian coffee/espresso maker, lined the back of the building. It seemed the DiMarcos did everything well and with distinction. Giuseppe had named the gallery Sofia after his late wife. Curator of the Sofia DiMarco collection would look good on Chloe's resume and help with her ultimate goal of opening her own gallery in Philadelphia.

"Do you want a latte?" Francesca asked.

"That sounds wonderful." As Francesca headed to the break room, Chloe settled into one of the comfortable desk chairs they'd brought from the offices. Giuseppe had had his workers bring in a temporary desk where two laptops now rested.

Hearing the door open, she looked over as Matteo walked in. His rugged good looks and his confident stride made her pulse jump. Today he wore an open-collared blue dress shirt, untucked, faded jeans that molded to his muscular legs, and black loafers worn without socks.

Smiling, she stood to greet him. He was her employer's grandson and she had to maintain a good relationship with him. Besides, they'd only shared a kiss. Not a big deal. The rapid beating of her heart painted a different picture. The kiss had been a very big deal, at least to her.

"*Buongiorno*, Chloe," he said in the deep, musical baritone that made warmth coalesce in her stomach and lower.

"Good morning. Or rather *buongiorno* to you too. I'm trying to use the Italian phrases I learned but my language skills are pathetic."

He chuckled. "Many Italians, especially in the tourist areas, speak English, so you shouldn't have a problem communicating."

"I know, but it's good to learn another language."

"It is." He looked around. "I see you've been busy. Are things to your liking? Do you need anything?"

"This is a beautiful structure, perfect for showing your grandmother's collection. The pieces are exquisite. Your grandfather has been very generous, giving us everything we need. I think it's wonderful he plans to donate the admission fees to charity."

Francesca came in holding two large ceramic cups. Her brown eyes widened when she saw Matteo.

"Signore DiMarco," she said, a reverent tone to her voice.

"Good morning, Francesca," he said in English. "It looks like you and Chloe have been working hard."

Francesca blushed and said something in rapid Italian.

"Glad you're enjoying your work," Matteo said in English. "As a courtesy to Chloe, we should speak English."

"Yes, of course," Francesca said.

Chloe expected the young woman to curtsy to Matteo.

"Would you like some coffee, Matteo?" Chloe asked.

He held up a hand. "No, thanks. I'm on my way to Rome. I have a function tonight I must attend."

Chloe should have been relieved Matteo would be away where he wouldn't be a temptation to her. Instead, she felt…deprived.

His gaze drifted to her mouth. The spark that lit his eyes told her he hadn't forgotten their kiss. Chloe gripped her coffee cup and took a large sip, coughing a little as the hot liquid burned a trail down her throat.

He frowned. “Are you okay?”

She waved a hand. “I didn’t realize how hot the coffee is.”

They stared at each other for several heat-inducing seconds, then he looked at his watch. “I must be going. Ciao, Chloe. Ciao, Francesca.”

“Ciao,” the women said in unison.

Then he was gone, taking some of the brightness with him.

Francesca muttered something in Italian.

“What?” Chloe said.

“Sorry,” Francesca said in English. “Signore DiMarco is, how you say in America, smokin’.”

Chloe laughed. “Smokin’ is the word for him.”

Francesca’s brown eyes gleamed. “Signore DiMarco thinks you are smokin’ too.”

Embarrassment tightened Chloe’s chest and warmed her face. She turned away and pretended to study one of the computer entries.

* * *

THAT EVENING, after a light dinner of roasted chicken and grilled vegetables, eaten alone on the patio, Chloe relaxed on the velvet-covered chaise in her spacious room, painted in shades of beige and white, the furniture heavy and ornate. Priceless antiques filled the room, an art historian’s dream. She switched on the TV, prepared for a quiet night.

Matteo invaded her thoughts, as he had all day. In one

day, he'd brought a vitality with him she'd never experienced. She wondered how long he'd be away. Trying without much success to push aside thoughts of him, she focused on the TV, changing channels until she settled on what looked like an entertainment show, much like "Entertainment Tonight" back in the States. Listening intently to the Italian commentary while attempting to match the words with the pictures, she froze when she heard "Matteo DiMarco."

A shot of Matteo with a sexy brunette who clung to him like paint on canvas flashed on. Chloe jumped off the chaise to peer closer at the TV, trying to read the Italian scroll along the bottom of the screen. From what she could ascertain, Matteo and the beauty attended a gala together that night. Dressed in a tuxedo, his dark hair slicked back and a hipster scruff on his face, Matteo's overt sexuality exploded onto the screen. The man could have found overwhelming success as an actor or model. The woman with him wore a skintight black dress with a plunging neckline that exposed most of her very large, no doubt surgically enhanced, breasts.

Chloe bit her lip against her unkind thoughts. She had no right to put the woman down. Yet, she couldn't stop the jealousy that cut her like a sculptor's chisel. She grabbed the remote and clicked off the TV, then threw the remote onto the bed. "Who Matteo DiMarco dates is no concern of yours, Chloe Decker," she said to the quiet room.

It had been three years since her fiancé died in that horrendous car accident, three years of mourning, of being without a man. No wonder she found herself drawn to Matteo. Maybe he would be the man to wake her up after Rob, but he would only be a distraction. Matteo couldn't be boyfriend material. According to the gossip rags, Matteo DiMarco was a player with lots of women. Definitely not the man for her.

CHAPTER 6

A full week had passed since the day she'd met Matteo in Ravello. Chloe knew he'd come back from Rome because she'd heard the roar of his car's engine the day after she'd seen him on TV. He hadn't joined her and Giuseppe for dinner or come to see her at work. She told herself the less she saw of Matteo DiMarco, the less chance she'd fall for his smooth-talking ways.

She sat on the patio finishing her breakfast of warm rolls with butter, and strong latte. Sipping her drink, her gaze wandered to the flowers that grew in abundance down to the Mediterranean, glittering turquoise far below. A small, twisted tree hung over the water and formed a perfect setting for the scene of splendor spread before her. She wished she were a good enough artist to capture the achingly beautiful panorama.

"Good morning, Chloe."

At Matteo's deep rumble, Chloe started, splashing coffee onto her hand. Wiping the coffee with a napkin, she turned slowly. Delicious shivers ran over her as she met his golden gaze. Her eyes trailed his body. Wearing close-fitting jeans, and a tan shirt, opened at the neck with the sleeves rolled up, he presented the picture of macho style.

"Sorry, Chloe. I didn't mean to startle you."

"I was in my own world, wrapped up in the remarkable scene before me."

He sat and grabbed a linen napkin off the table to drape on his lap. Pulling a cup closer, he poured himself coffee from the carafe set in the center of the glass-topped table.

Glancing toward the gardens and the sea, he said, "Sometimes I get so used to the view I forget to admire its beauty."

"I could never get tired of looking at it."

He buttered a roll, his movements graceful and sensual. She wondered what his hands would feel like touching her, rubbing her skin. Watching his throat muscles work as he chewed made her gulp the last of her coffee and clutch the cup like a lifeline against her traitorous thoughts. He looked up and found her staring.

Face burning, trying to keep her expression neutral, Chloe grabbed the carafe and poured herself a half cup of coffee, topping it off with steamed milk.

"I've missed you," he said. "Many things at work needed my attention."

"I've been busy at the gallery." She'd never let him know she'd missed him too, or that he intrigued her.

One of the maids bustled in with a fresh pot of coffee, more steamed milk, and a basket of rolls. When Matteo held out the basket to Chloe, she shook her head. "I've eaten too many of the rolls already. Your cook, Lucia, does an incredible job."

He ate while she enjoyed her latte, slid furtive glances at him, and pretended to be absorbed in her surroundings. Like a painting from a master, what she really wanted to do was stare at him.

"Today is no work for you, right?" he said, breaking the silence.

Nodding, she turned to him. "I thought I'd explore the town a little more today." She smiled. "And try some new gelato flavors."

He stood. "We've both been working hard and we need a break. Come with me today to the Amalfi Coast. We'll have lunch at Portofino."

Drive the twisting, narrow roads of the Amalfi Coast with Matteo again? The part of her that craved adventure said *yes*. The fearful part of her, the one that worried about accidents, said *no*.

"In your Maserati?" she blurted.

"What else would I drive?"

She chewed her lip. "I want to see more of the Amalfi Coast and Portofino, but these narrow roads scare me." She looked down at her white Capris, flat-heeled tan leather sandals, and pink tank top. "I've heard Portofino is very upscale. I'm not dressed for it."

He bent to lean close. "You are beautiful, as always. And I will drive carefully. Come."

She really wanted to be with him. It would mean riding in his fast car over twisting roads. One wrong turn could plunge them over the cliffs. Forcing herself to focus on him rather than her fears, she nodded. "I'd love to go to Portofino with you." She held out her hand and allowed him to help her stand.

He skimmed fingers along her face in a soft caress. She shivered as he led her from the patio. She wondered if she had more to fear from the winding roads of Amalfi or from the sexual energy of Matteo.

CHAPTER 7

As they traveled along the narrow roads and hairpin turns of the Amalfi Coast, Matteo drove carefully, prompting horn blowing from impatient drivers behind him. Chloe relaxed slightly, warmed by Matteo's consideration in keeping his speed down. Below them, small villages dotted the cliffs leading to the Mediterranean. The turquoise sea sat like a jewel in the crown of this playground of gods and emperors. Wild flowers clung to the sides of the cliffs and swayed in the gentle sweet-scented breeze.

"It's almost too beautiful to bear," Chloe said.

Matteo chuckled. "You're not so afraid now?"

"I'm still afraid, but I'm more in awe."

Matteo turned onto one of the meandering roads leading toward the sea. "Portofino."

He maneuvered the car down the road clogged with vehicles of all sizes competing for space. Flags in a riot of colors hung from brightly painted houses that straddled the sides of the cliffs like rock climbers desperately trying not to fall. Sailboats bobbed in the green water of a marina, the emerald of the water competing with the turquoise of the sea. Pedestrians jostled for space on the crowded sidewalks. Cars were parked in every available spot, with other cars driving slowly by, looking for parking places.

"You'll never find a place to park," Chloe said.

"No problem." Matteo pulled onto a road leading to a marina and waved to the guard manning the small booth at the entrance. He drove a short distance and parked in front of a white yacht that looked big enough to house a family of ten. Chloe recognized the flag flying from the mast as the coat of arms of the DiMarco family.

She turned to Matteo. "This is your yacht?"

He nodded. "Lunch should be ready."

"We're eating on your yacht?"

"Of course." He turned off the ignition, exited the car, and came around to her side.

Feeling like a country bumpkin on her first trip to the city, Chloe slid out of the car and stared up at the huge ship, named the *Sofia*. "It's named for your grandmother."

"My father bought the yacht soon after my parents married." Matteo chuckled. "My mother insisted he name it after her, Valentina, but he refused."

Matteo put his hand on the small of Chloe's back and led her up the wooden walkway to the deck, where a crew member in uniform waited.

"Signore DiMarco," the man said, tipping his hat. He said something in Italian and led them along the main deck and up narrow steps to a second deck where a white-clothed table set with china and crystal waited. The ends of the tablecloth waved gently in the breeze, little welcoming flags.

Chloe walked to the railing to gaze out over the harbor and the magnificence spread before them. The sun beat down on her bare shoulders, warming her like a lover's touch. She sighed and drank in the scene before her.

Matteo came up behind her. She inhaled his subtle scent of sandalwood. She needed to resist his pull. For now, in this mystical place of beauty, sun, and flowers she would put aside the sadness that had plagued her the past few years and enjoy this moment with this man.

Someone spoke in Italian behind them, and she heard the sound of chairs scraping the wooden deck.

"Come," Matteo said. "Our lunch is ready."

The man in uniform who'd greeted them stood smiling by the table. After they sat, the man clapped his hands, and waiters brought out platters of lobster, whitefish, pasta with marinara sauce, and grilled vegetables.

One of the waiters opened a bottle of chilled white wine and presented the cork to Matteo. After Matteo proclaimed the wine acceptable, the waiter poured each of them a glass.

When the others left, Matteo lifted his glass. "To your beauty."

"Thank you." She touched her glass to his. "I'd rather drink to the beauty of Portofino and the Amalfi Coast."

They ate in comfortable silence. The exquisite food, wine, and surroundings, but most of all, the alluring man with her, wrapped Chloe's heart in a blend of excitement and contentment she hadn't known for a very long time.

Matteo reached across the table and put his hand over

hers. "Tell me, Chloe Decker, is there a man at home waiting for you?"

Some of her joy evaporated into the flower-scented air. She slid her hand from his, set down her fork, and glanced away.

"I'm sorry, Chloe. I didn't mean to upset you. What is it?"

She turned and met his concerned gaze. She twisted her fingers around the stem of her wine glass as if the act could give her strength. With a deep breath, she said, "I was engaged to a wonderful man. We'd been together since high school and planned a future with each other."

"What happened?" he asked softly.

"He died three years ago in a car accident." She gave a weak smile. "He liked to drive fast."

"Ah. So that is the friend who died while driving fast."

"For the first six months after Rob died, I couldn't even drive my own car. I'm trying to get over my fears."

She sipped her wine and glanced out over the water. "Rob and I had our lives planned out. I taught school while he earned his Master of Fine Arts degree. We hoped to one day run our own gallery."

"What about you?" Matteo asked quietly. "What did you want?"

Chloe turned back to him with a wry smile. "I wanted to earn my Masters too, but I put that aside for Rob. Now that I have my degree, I plan to one day have my own gallery."

"A worthy plan," he said. "You still love this Rob?"

"He will always have a place in my heart."

True, Rob would always be special. She missed male

companionship. Maybe the time had come to open her heart again. Fear gripped her anew. To open her heart would be opening up to hurt again.

"Chloe?"

She met Matteo's gaze.

"I can compete with other men," he said. "I can't compete with a ghost."

"Compete?" She took a fortifying sip of wine. The cool slide of it down her throat did little to drown out the feelings of confusion, anticipation, and yearning that spilled over her.

Matteo took her hand, and with his thumb, drew a lazy circle in her palm. "You must know I'm attracted to you."

Heat pumped through her veins until common sense cooled her. She moved her hand from his. "You're a charmer, that's for sure. I know your reputation, Matteo. I've seen the pictures. I won't be one of your conquests."

Hurt tightened his features. "Don't believe everything you see and hear."

Disappointment that their beautiful day was ruined swirled through Chloe like the seabirds that glided through the sky above them.

Not speaking, they topped off their meal with a tiramisu and strong espresso. On the ride back, Matteo said little other than point out sights of interest. Chloe stared straight ahead, afraid to look down at the sea far below, waiting like a shark for them to run off the road and into its watery jaws.

CHAPTER 8

When Matteo pulled up to the circular drive in front of the palazzo, the door opened, and a middle-aged woman, her long blonde hair streaked with golden highlights, came out. Arms folded and eyes narrowed, she watched Chloe alight from the car.

"Ciao, Mama," Matteo said, going up to the woman and giving her a kiss on the cheek.

Chloe approached the woman, a smile on her face, prepared to meet Matteo's mother.

"Mama," he said in English. "This is Chloe Decker. She is the art expert curating Grandmother's collection. Chloe, my mother, Valentina DiMarco."

"Nice to meet you, Mrs. DiMarco." Chloe held out her hand.

Matteo's mother took Chloe's hand in a limp shake before releasing her quickly, as if Chloe had a disease. Her eyes, like chips of frozen black glass, scanned Chloe. "I have heard about you from my father-in-law. He seems to think highly of you."

Apparently, Valentina DiMarco didn't agree. With a smile plastered on her face, Chloe stepped back. "I'd better go in. It's been a long day."

As she entered the house, she heard Matteo and his mother raise their voices in what sounded like an argument. Whatever the dynamics between the two, they weren't Chloe's problems.

She had a more immediate problem. She was falling for Matteo. The thought terrified her.

* * *

"WHAT ARE you doing with that woman?" Matteo's mother poked her finger in his chest. "She is nobody, an American. She is no good for you."

Matteo gently removed his mother's finger. "Who I choose to spend time with is none of your concern, Mama. Chloe is an intelligent and talented woman whose company I enjoy. She's done a remarkable job already on the collection. We're lucky to have her."

"You and that grandfather of yours, taken by a pretty face." She lifted her chin. "You are a DiMarco, from one of the oldest, most noble families in Italy. Keep those stupid women you are seen with. When you marry, it must be to someone worthy of the DiMarco name."

He frowned. "Marry?"

"I saw the way you looked at the Decker woman. She's not one of us. I will not stand for it."

He moved closer until they were nose-to-nose. "If I marry, it will be to a woman of my choosing."

She snorted. "Like you chose Ingrid? She showed her true colors seducing your uncle away from his wife."

"That was a long time ago, Mama. Do not mention it again."

He stalked into the house, not looking back at her. His social climbing mother had tried unsuccessfully through the years to pair him with one European princess after another. He'd never succumbed to her machinations, and he wouldn't now. His mother didn't scare him.

His growing feelings for Chloe did.

THREE DAYS after their drive to Portofino, Chloe and Matteo, along with Giuseppe, sat in front of one of the computers in the new gallery. Francesca sat at the other computer ready to take notes. The cataloging had been going so quickly and smoothly Chloe knew her time here would soon end. She stole a glance at Matteo, next to her. She hadn't seen much of him since their lunch on the yacht. He'd joined her and his grandfather for dinner a few times, but disappeared soon after eating. Giuseppe told her Matteo was busy putting together a contract for a new client.

Finding it hard to concentrate with Matteo so near, she cleared her throat and focused on the job at hand. "I thought it would make the gallery experience more personal for the visitors if we knew the background of each piece," she said, with a nod at Giuseppe.

"Signore DiMarco," she continued. "I know many of these pieces meant a lot to your wife. As we go through them, if you can give us a little story, Francesca will record it and we'll have the stories printed up with the artifacts."

The elderly man grinned. "That is a very good idea, Chloe. My mind, it isn't what it used to be. I hope I can remember."

"Who are you fooling, Grandfather?" Matteo said. "Your mind is as sharp as ever."

Chloe and Francesca laughed. Then Chloe brought up the first item on the computer. "This blue Murano vase is exquisite. We want to make it the centerpiece of the collection. What can you tell us about it?"

Giuseppe's eyes misted and he looked away, as if seeing something far off. Finally, he spoke. "Sofia and I bought it on our honeymoon in Venice sixty years ago. Sofia loved the vase. I could not deny her."

"That's so romantic." Chloe sighed and met Matteo's gaze. His eyes sparked gold fire. Every cell in her body burned as liquid heat flowed through her.

The soft clicking of keys as Francesca entered the information about the vase tore Chloe from her sensual cloud.

They worked for another hour until Giuseppe tired. Matteo helped his grandfather stand, then turned to Chloe. Leaning close, he whispered, "I've missed you. Have dinner with me tonight in Ravello?"

Aware of Francesca and Giuseppe looking on with interest, Chloe nodded.

At Matteo's bright smile, her stomach fluttered. She played with fire, flirting with him.

Maybe for once in her life, she wanted to play with fire.

CHAPTER 9

Chloe and Matteo had dinner at an outdoor café in the shadows of the Duomo, or Cathedral, of Ravello. The setting sun cast a golden glow over the white edifice of the Cathedral, built in the eleventh century.

Chloe finished her strawberry gelato and leaned back in her chair with a contented sigh. She scanned the colorful piazza, filled with tourists and natives on this warm summer night. Feeling Matteo's stare, her gaze slid to him. Awareness flashed from his eyes, inciting a response low in her belly.

A stray memory touched her with sadness, and she looked down at the table.

Matteo touched her chin with his fingers until their gazes met. "What is wrong, Chloe?"

She rubbed a finger along the rim of her half-empty wine glass. "Rob and I dreamed of traveling to Italy someday. He would have loved it here." She sipped some wine before continuing. "It's been three years. I've tried to move on. I feel badly he never got to see this."

Maybe the softness in Matteo's eyes or perhaps the wine caused her to let down her guard, but she wanted to tell him how she felt. "I haven't so much as looked at another man. Until you. I'm attracted to you, Matteo, and it scares me."

His features gentle, he leaned closer. "It's right that you have good memories of this Rob. You are a young woman, filled with life. Any man would be glad to call you his. Our attraction to each other in no way takes from the love you felt for your fiancé."

Chloe looked into his eyes and fell deeper. "Matteo, you're an exciting, sexy guy. You're smart, and kind to your grandfather. Fun to be with. We barely know each other. You and I are from different countries, different worlds."

His nostrils flared and he shook his head. As if he needed something to do, he poured them each more wine from the bottle on the table. They were silent while they sipped their drinks. Finally, he set his glass onto the table and met her gaze again.

"I deserve your doubts about me. I keep a high profile for the benefit of my company. Those models and actresses with me need the publicity of being with a DiMarco. The gossip magazine our company owns needs the readership. It's a business deal for me and the women."

He took one of her hands in his and stroked her palm, sending shivers up her arm.

"I'm not anything like my public image," he said. "I, too, have my own story."

"I'd like to hear it."

He released her and settled back in his chair. "When I was twenty," he began. "I fell in love with another student at my university. Ingrid was Swedish, blonde, beautiful, a talented artist. I wanted to marry her. I brought her home to meet my family." He swallowed and looked away, as if the memory pained him.

"What happened?" Chloe asked gently.

He faced her again, his features a mask, devoid of emotion. "Ingrid wasn't what she seemed. She wanted money, and lots of it. I hadn't yet come into my inheritance. She seduced my Uncle Santino, a man thirty years her senior, a man with a wife and grown children." Matteo released a bitter laugh. "It wasn't hard to seduce Santino. He had several mistresses at the time, still does. He left his wife and married Ingrid."

Matteo's mouth settled into a tight line. "After Ingrid, I vowed to never expose my heart to another woman, or to trust again."

"I'm so sorry, Matteo. What a terrible thing to happen."

He shrugged. "What I'm trying to tell you is that I've guarded my heart all these years. Then I met you. You're different from any woman I've known. You're good and kind and smart. And real, without pretense."

Fear and hope collided in her chest, taking her breath. "It's too soon, Matteo. You and I just met."

"My grandparents knew each other two weeks before he asked her to marry him."

Chloe choked on her wine. "Marry?"

He laughed and waved a hand in dismissal. "Don't

worry. I'll take it easy. I like you. You're very *simpatico*. Let us see where this takes us."

She pressed a palm to her stomach where frenzied butterflies had taken up residence. "I don't know."

"I only ask for a chance." He smiled. "Come, we'll take a walk in the Villa Rufolo Gardens before we go back."

As they strolled the lush gardens of Villa Rufolo, he took her hand in his. She didn't pull away, didn't want to. Being with him warmed her all over and made everything around them more alive. Even the lavish display of colors in the famous gardens seemed brighter with Matteo so near. She'd loved Rob, and they'd had a comfortable relationship. The sex had been good, if not exciting. She'd never felt on edge with Rob like she did with Matteo, her whole body singing, waiting for something thrilling. She'd never come so alive with Rob, as she did with Matteo. And she'd never wanted Rob with a hunger that threatened to overwhelm her.

She could no longer deny she craved Matteo's touch, a look from him, his voice, his laugh. She wanted to make love with him.

A short while later, as dark descended, still fighting her desire, she buckled herself into the Maserati for the ride back to the villa. Driving the sharp turns in the darkness sent fear spiraling through her, and she gripped the edge of the leather seat. Matteo slowed down.

He drew up in front of the villa and cut the engine. She waited for him to open her door. Used to opening her own doors, she liked his Old-World manners. The thought that her work would soon be done and she'd leave formed a heavy stone of regret in her chest.

He cupped her elbow as they walked toward the door. When they reached it, Matteo turned her to face him. He leaned closer until they were a whisper apart. Chloe forgot to breathe. He brushed his fingers along her collarbone and down to the flower pendant she wore. Her insides trembled.

Lifting the pendant, he rubbed a finger over it. "I will always remember how you looked that first day in Ravello when you bought this. Your beauty shone, calling to me."

With a low murmur, he gathered her to him. Then his lips were on hers, coaxing, teasing, seducing her to give in to her desire. She linked her arms around his neck and opened to him. Their tongues danced in an erotic rhythm that sent fierce, desperate need through her.

He backed her up against the door and aligned his body so it touched her in all the right places. His hardness told her he wanted her as much as she wanted him. She felt hot, restless, her breasts tight, her nipples pushing against the silk of her bra.

His deep, drugging kiss claimed and devoured her. Moaning, she pressed closer, wanting to mold her body to his, to never let him go. Heat built in her, a fire only Matteo could extinguish.

He left her mouth to trail scorching kisses along her jawline and down her throat, eliciting more moans from deep inside her. With deft movements, he slid his hands beneath her top to caress her breasts through the thin fabric of her bra. His fingers burned her flesh. Boneless and needy, she clung to him. Liquid fire raced through her veins.

"Chloe," he whispered against her mouth. "I want you."

His words gave life to the fear that lurked just beneath the surface of her mind. She couldn't do this. Oh, but she wanted him.

She pushed away and adjusted her tank top. "I can't, Matteo. I can't."

Hands trembling, she turned the doorknob and opened the door, slipping inside. She hurried to the safety of her room. Once inside, she threw herself on the bed and let the tears flow. Tears of frustration, anxiety, guilt, fear. And need.

CHAPTER 10

Chloe and Francesca worked hard over the next two weeks to finish the cataloging and design the layout for the exhibit. Since sharing that hot kiss with Matteo after their dinner in Ravello, she'd seen little of him. The rare nights he attended dinner with her and his grandfather, Matteo let her know by his looks, his attention, that he still wanted her. She knew he spent long hours on negotiations on a contract the company desperately wanted.

She tossed and turned most nights, filled with sexual frustration. She and Rob had enjoyed a steady sex life, and Chloe missed that. She missed the physical connection with another person. The emotional part of her feared what would happen to her heart if she allowed herself to love Matteo.

They'd finished cataloging the artifacts and had a plan for the placement of the objects. Chloe had called a meeting this morning with Matteo and Giuseppe to go through the files and present them with their ideas. Now, waiting in the gallery, apprehension tightened her stomach. She hoped the DiMarcos would be pleased at what she and Francesca had accomplished and that they'd agree to their suggestions.

The door opened, and Matteo and Giuseppe entered, the elderly man leaning on his cane with one hand, and holding onto his grandson with the other.

"Buongiorno," Chloe said. She gestured to two comfortable chairs in front of the desk.

As the men moved into the room, Chloe's gaze caught Matteo's. Something sizzled and crackled between them. Face hot, she glanced at Giuseppe and Francesca, but neither seemed to notice the sensual fireworks.

Once everyone took seats, Chloe brought up the files on her computer, explaining to the men how they'd cataloged each piece. When she finished, Giuseppe smiled and sat back in his chair.

"*Molto bene*, Chloe. Very good." Tears formed in his eyes. "My Sofia would be extremely happy to see the loving care you have given her collection."

With a relieved breath, Chloe put her hand over her heart. "Thank you, Signore DiMarco. I'm so glad you're pleased. I'm honored you chose me to work on this amazing collection."

"My grandfather is right," Matteo said. "You and Francesca have done an outstanding job."

"Thank you," Chloe and Francesca said at the same time.

Tired of sitting, Chloe stood. She pulled the other laptop toward her and opened it, clicked a few keys, and turned the computer to face the others. "Francesca and I did a layout of the building, and we've come up with ideas to showcase the objects. Let me show you."

Pointing at the computer screen, she explained the best way to display the artifacts. She loved arranging the beautiful pieces virtually and couldn't wait to do it physically.

When she finished her presentation, she looked expectantly at the men. Matteo nodded. "Perfect."

Giuseppe's weathered face broke out in a grin. "We will go with your plans."

Chloe's heart raced, and pleasure radiated heat through her. "Thank you. There's one more thing I'd like to suggest." She folded her arms across her chest. "Why not have a color catalog printed up with pictures of each piece and the story attached to it? You could open a small gift shop and sell the catalog along with other art-related items. I think people would love it, and it would bring in more money for your charities."

"Yes! Wonderful!" Giuseppe said.

"I'm pleased you like our ideas," Chloe said.

Francesca smiled. "It has been my pleasure to work with Chloe and the DiMarco family."

Matteo's phone rang. He looked at the screen, then at his grandfather. "One of our lawyers. I have to take it." He headed outside.

When he'd gone, Giuseppe looked at Francesca. "Could you please bring us some coffee?"

"Si, Signore." She flounced out of the room.

"Chloe," Giuseppe said when they were alone.

She met the elderly man's gaze.

"You have done a good job for us."

"Thank you, Signore. That means a lot to me."

A teasing gleam came into his eyes. "You mean a lot to my grandson."

She sank into her chair. "What?"

"You must know he cares for you. And I know you care for him."

"Is it that obvious?"

Giuseppe nodded. "My grandson needs a woman like you in his life."

"His reputation—"

Giuseppe waved a hand. "Matteo is no playboy. It is all a show for publicity, for the women and for our company. You would be good for him."

"Signore, I appreciate what you are trying to do, but this is between Matteo and me. What's more, I have to go home. My parents and family are in Philadelphia. That's where I belong."

He gave her a sly smile. "Perhaps we can find a way to make you want to stay."

CHAPTER 11

Over the next week and a half, Chloe and Francesca worked with the contractors to set up the exhibit and place the items. Each evening, Chloe had dinner with Matteo and Giuseppe. Matteo treated her cordially, but nothing more. She began to think she and his grandfather had misinterpreted Matteo's interest in her.

Now, after days of physical labor, she stood in the main gallery and rubbed her aching lower back. As she looked around at the modern, spacious room, pride flowed through her. The fading sunlight slanting through the Palladian windows gleamed on the blue Murano vase, the centerpiece of the exhibit, sending prisms of blue, gold, and green reflecting off the white walls.

Giuseppe had written her a glowing letter of recommendation, which netted her an interview at a prestigious gallery in Philadelphia.

The day after tomorrow, she'd leave Ravello, the fairy-tale place of dreams.

She'd leave Matteo.

Regret pressed against her chest, stifling her breath. Maybe she should have had a fling with him, gotten him out of her system. Something told her she'd never get Matteo DiMarco out of her system.

* * *

THAT NIGHT, as they were finishing dinner, Matteo turned to her. "Let's walk in the gardens."

Giuseppe concentrated on sipping his espresso and looked away, but Chloe knew he hung onto Matteo's every word.

"Okay," she said. "It's a beautiful night. I'd like a walk."

As Matteo helped her from her chair, Giuseppe winked at her. Chloe's face burned.

Matteo placed his hand on the small of her back as they strolled along the cobblestone walkway. The flowers that lined the path guided their way, colorful and fragrant guardians.

"It's so mysterious and beautiful here," she said. "I'll hold these memories close to warm me during Philadelphia's cold and dreary winters."

He took her hand and turned her to face him. Skimming fingers over her face, he said, "You don't have to go back. Stay here."

With a low gasp, she pulled away. "Stay here? And do what?"

He grabbed her hand again. "Let's sit."

He led her to a stone bench in the rose garden.

Bacchus looked down on them from his pedestal, as if urging them to partake in illicit delights.

Matteo took both Chloe's hands in his. His eyes, shadowed in the darkness, seemed to bore into hers.

"I don't want you to go, Chloe. There is something between us. I've tried to stay away from you, to give you time. I didn't want to pressure you. You leave soon and time is running out."

"I love it here, Matteo, but my home is in Philadelphia. My family and friends are there, and it's where I hope to make a career. I have an interview at one of the top galleries next week. I can't up and move to another country."

His eyes searched hers. "My grandfather and I would like to hire you to run the exhibit."

"I thought you hired a retired museum director for that."

"She didn't want to work full time so we'll offer her a part-time position. With what you've done, we believe our gallery will be a great success. That means more money for our charities. We may want to add to the collection, and we'll need your expert help for that. We can pay you well, and you can continue to live here. You and I can be together. We'll have time to explore this thing between us."

She pulled free and narrowed her eyes. "Did your grandfather put you up to this?"

"He mentioned it to me, but I'd already considered it." Matteo grasped her shoulders and pulled her closer. "I'm falling in love with you. I don't want to lose you."

Fear, anxiety, and joy mixed into a tight ball in her

stomach. "I care for you, Matteo. This seems impossible when we live an ocean apart."

He gripped her shoulders tighter. "Chloe, I understand your reluctance to move a world away, but we can make it work."

Her mind scattered with conflicting thoughts, and she broke free of him and stood. Hugging herself, she walked down the narrow path that led through the rose garden. Clouds scudded across a moonless sky. Far below, the inky black Mediterranean lapped gently against the shore.

She'd given up her ambitions for Rob. Putting her own MFA plans on hold, she taught school and saved money for the house they'd eventually buy together. Rob had a teaching assistant job at the university while he earned his MFA. After they married, they'd planned for her to continue teaching while he worked at one of the galleries, with the goal of opening his own someday. She'd squashed her dreams and dutifully went along with Rob's plans. She couldn't give up her dreams for a man again.

She heard leaves rustle behind her and knew Matteo approached. He slid his arms around her waist and pulled her against him. She rested her head on his chest. He offered her a chance to live a new dream. She had to go home, had to work on her career on her own terms. She could give in to her craving for him, could love him for the short time they had.

She turned in his arms and stroked her fingers over his chiseled cheekbones and down to the light stubble on his face. "I have to do things my way, Matteo. I don't know if I'm ready to risk my future on the possibility of a relationship with you. Or any man right now."

Placing her hands on his shoulders, she stood on tiptoe to brush her lips lightly over his. “I want you, Matteo. Give me this night with you.”

He cupped her face. His intense gaze held her. “I want more than one night with you.”

“It’s all I can promise now.”

“You are sure? You want this?”

“Yes.”

* * *

Early morning sunlight slipped into Chloe’s room, touching the corners in gold. She lay on her back and stared at the ceiling and the small crystal chandelier hanging from an ornate medallion. She would miss this luxurious room with its sitting area and ensuite bathroom. She’d miss the man who slept next to her even more.

Matteo stirred, and she turned to him. He opened his gold-brown eyes. “Buongiorno, cara mia.”

“Good morning, Matteo,” she whispered.

He gathered her into his arms. She snuggled against his hard chest. Making love with him through the night had been the most incredible experience of her life. A skilled and giving lover, Matteo had brought her to heights she’d never thought possible. She wanted more of him.

“Make love to me, Matteo.”

CHAPTER 12

Bags packed, Chloe waited in her room for the DiMarco chauffeur to collect her. He'd drive her to Rome where she'd booked a hotel room for the night. Tomorrow she'd fly back to the States.

Afraid she might be sick from nervousness and sadness, she pressed a hand to her stomach. She caught sight of herself in the large beveled mirror. Despite her use of makeup, the dark shadows under her eyes were stark reminders she hadn't had much sleep the past forty-eight hours.

She and Matteo had spent two glorious nights making sweet, passionate love. The more time she spent with him, the more she didn't want to leave.

Now her heart would break all over again.

She was in love with Matteo.

He never said he loved her.

"Ciao, Signore DiMarco." Chloe hugged Giuseppe as they stood at the front of the villa. Nunzio, standing nearby, held the passenger car door open for Chloe. Giuseppe had come to mean so much to her. She smiled as she pulled away. "I appreciate your giving me this chance."

"I wish you could stay for the gallery opening in one week," Giuseppe said. "I'm sure we will be a great success thanks to your talents and hard work."

"I wish I could stay, too, but I have that interview next week in Philadelphia. When I applied to the gallery online and sent your letter of recommendation, they got back to me quickly. That wouldn't have happened without your help." She looked around at the sun-dappled trees and flowers and the stately marble and stone villa with its red-tiled roof. "I will miss you and your beautiful home."

"I believe you will miss someone else more," Giuseppe said.

She looked away. "Matteo and I have our own lives."

As if she'd conjured him up, the front door opened and Matteo came out. They'd said their goodbyes in the bedroom earlier, she choking back tears, and Matteo with a stoic expression on his elegant features.

Her heart leapt at the sight of him now, and she swallowed. His hair was damp as if he'd just stepped from the shower. A white T-shirt stretched across his muscled chest, and close-fitting jeans showcased his long legs. Images of running her fingers over the firm muscles of his chest swirled through her. She wanted to devour him.

He strode to her and gripped her shoulders. "Chloe, please don't leave. We'll work things out."

At the pleading in his eyes, her heart broke a little. She knew what she had to do.

"Being here with you has been the most wonderful experience of my life. I have to go back. To my real world." She waved a hand. "None of this is real, not to me. I don't belong here."

"You belong with me."

She blinked back tears. "Please. I have to go."

He pulled her to him and took her lips in a hungry kiss that shattered her control. She forgot about Giuseppe and Nunzio standing nearby. Only Matteo existed. Her soul, her heart, belonged to him. With a moan, she wrapped her arms around his neck and kissed him with all the pent-up frustration and love she couldn't voice.

With effort, she broke free and slid into the car before Matteo could see her tears. As they drove away, she looked back to find Matteo watching her, his face filled with devastation.

Her tears flowed freely.

CHAPTER 13

Chloe sat at a small table at Trevi Fountain in Rome. She'd arrived a few hours ago from Ravello. After checking into her hotel and refreshing herself, she'd walked to Trevi, only blocks away. She'd already tossed in the requisite coins—one for success in business, one that she would return to Rome, and one that she'd find love.

Her thoughts flew to Matteo. Had she found love with him, only to throw it away? Her family would understand if she decided to stay in Italy. In her heart, she knew Rob would understand. He'd want her to be happy. Her own fear kept her from taking a leap of faith. If she gave her heart to Matteo, only to lose him, she might never recover.

She lifted her wine glass and sipped. King Neptune stared at her from his place on the fountain. He seemed to say, *You know what you want. Take a chance for once in your life, Chloe.*

Setting down her glass, she closed her eyes and rubbed the flower pendant she wore. Like a talisman, the pendant calmed her and brought forth images of Matteo laughing, smiling, his eyes dark with desire when he looked at her. *I don't know what to do. I love Matteo. This would be so much easier if he said he loved me.*

When she opened her eyes again, a shaft of golden-pink light from the setting sun shone on King Neptune. She smiled. *Thanks, water-boy.*

She would go back to Ravello, take a chance on Matteo, take a chance on love again. Decision made, Chloe grabbed her purse and stood.

And came face-to-face with Matteo.

"I have found you," he said.

The joy that lit his eyes made hope churn through her. Feeling lightheaded, she sank onto her seat.

"How did you know I was here?" she said, her voice breathless.

He sat across from her and reached over the small table to grasp her hand. He raised her hand to his lips and planted a kiss on her palm. "The clerk at your hotel told me where to find you."

"What are you doing here, in Rome?"

Holding onto her hand, he leaned closer. "I came to tell you I love you, Chloe Decker."

The power of his words made her entire body tingle and tremble. The noisy piazza crowded with tourists enjoying the famous fountain faded into a joyous haze. Nothing else existed except her and the man she loved.

"You love me?" she finally managed.

He smiled that slow, sexy smile that took the air from her lungs.

"Of course, I love you. I have been stupid, Chloe. I almost let you go."

He moved his chair closer until their shoulders touched. "You've taught me what real love is. I can't imagine a world without you. Please don't walk away. I need you in my life. I don't want to keep you from your career. If you must go home to Philadelphia, we'll find a way to be together." A tortured look replaced the joy in his eyes. "Maybe you don't love me."

"Oh, Matteo." She wrapped her arms around his neck. "I do love you. I think I fell in love with you the minute I saw you at that vendor stand in Ravello."

An expression of wonder crossed his face. "My Chloe." He bent to take her lips in a tender kiss that promised a future of love and passion.

Finally, they pulled apart, their breathing ragged. He brushed his fingers over her face. "I will come to Philadelphia with you. Our company has offices in New York. I can work from there. I will do anything to make you happy, my Chloe."

She smiled at him. "Is that job offer in Ravello still open?"

"What are you saying?"

She touched his arm and felt his muscles tense. "I'd like to come home with you." The word *home* rolled off her tongue and filled her heart. She belonged here in Italy, with Matteo. Her heart had healed and she'd found a new life, because of the fateful letter she'd received all those months ago.

EPILOGUE

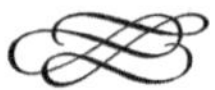

Ravello, six months later

Chloe stood in the vestibule of the ornate Cathedral of Ravello nervously clutching her bridal bouquet and waited for the music to herald the start of her wedding ceremony.

"You look beautiful, Chloe. Quit fidgeting," her mother, standing beside her, said.

"Your mother is right. I'm proud of you, sweetheart," her dad, on her other side, said.

She stood on tiptoe and gave each a kiss on the cheek. "Thanks, Mom, Dad."

Chloe's brothers, along with their families, were already seated in the church.

Giuseppe, between Valentina and Ingrid in the front pew, turned in his seat to smile at Chloe. She gave him a little wave. She loved the elderly man. As for Valentina and Ingrid, not so much. They'd worn sour looks on their faces earlier as they'd taken their seats. None of that mattered. Only Matteo mattered.

"You are stunning in that Valentino gown. Matteo won't know what hit him," Ellie, Chloe's best friend and maid-of-honor said, drawing her attention.

Chloe laughed and took calming breaths, running a hand down the side of the duchesse satin gown with the Swarovski crystal bodice. Weak sunlight streamed in through the stained-glass windows, bathing everything in pinks, blues, greens, and golds. A good omen. She lifted her left hand and turned it, letting the sunbeams glint on the facets of her diamond engagement ring. The large round diamond, with smaller diamonds surrounding it, had belonged to Sofia, Matteo's grandmother.

The gallery had proven a huge success, and Giuseppe planned to enlarge it and add more items. Chloe loved her work, but she loved Matteo and the life they planned together even more.

One of the ushers accompanied Chloe's mother down the aisle as the violinist played Schubert's *Ave Verum*. Chloe gripped her bouquet tighter. With a thumbs-up for Chloe, Ellie began her march along the white runner to the altar.

Then it was Chloe's turn. She threaded her arm through her father's. Her dad patted her hand and smiled at her. Bells pealed out as they started down the aisle. Chloe's attention focused on her handsome husband-to-be, waiting for her. Stunning in a custom tuxedo, Matteo's beauty stole her breath. The love shining in his eyes stole her heart and soul.

When she reached him, her dad placed her hand in

Matteo's and took his seat next to her mother. Together, Chloe and Matteo faced the priest. Matteo leaned down to whisper in her ear.

"You are the most beautiful woman I have ever seen," he said. "I love you more than life itself."

"I love you too, Matteo. I will forever."

They smiled at each other as the priest began the ceremony that would unite them forever into a picture-perfect life filled with love.

A life that started with a letter.

THE course of true love doesn't run smoothly for Chloe and Matteo. Read more of their story in Ravello Marriage Bargain (Amore Italiano Book 2)

RAVELLO MARRIAGE BARGAIN

AMORE ITALIANO BOOK 2

Cara Marsi

Published by The Painted Lady Press

United States of America

First Electronic Edition: October 2020

Cover by Harris Channing

Formatting by Aileen Fish

Edited by BKR Editing

Cover copy created by BlurbWriter.com

Art historian and curator Chloe Decker DiMarco never belonged in Ravello, Italy. Her whirlwind marriage should never have happened. The colors had quickly faded from the sunny Italian life she'd pictured for them, turned dark and muddy by rumors of infidelities, jealous ex-lovers, and a mother-in-law who would have preferred her precious son marry royalty instead of a barbarian American. Intimidated by the wealth and power of the DiMarcos, and lacking support from her husband, Chloe fled back to Philadelphia and hit the reset button on her life. But a two-year separation hasn't lessened the heat Matteo DiMarco ignites when he walks into her art gallery.

A man's wife should trust him. He shouldn't have to explain himself to her. But Matteo's grandfather is dying, and his last wish is to see Matteo and Chloe reunited. The machismo that's bred so deeply in Matteo isn't going to help him lure back the one woman who'd painted his world with joy. So he strikes a bargain: if she returns to Italy for a pretend reconciliation, he'll give her the divorce she wants.

But Chloe has a secret, one that could ruin the

picture-perfect plan. Is she willing to take a second-chance journey to love, to return to where it all began—to where it all ended so badly? Matteo has a face that could have been chiseled by Michelangelo; is his heart as hard and cold as a statue's, or is he willing to display a softer side? Is there any hope they can turn their marriage bargain into a priceless lifetime of love?

CHAPTER 1

Philadelphia, Pennsylvania

"Take your hands off my wife."

Chloe Decker DiMarco jumped back from the man who held her. She whirled, stomach churning, to the man standing in the doorway, his sculpted features tight. His baritone voice, tinged with his lyrical Italian accent, still dominated her dreams.

Pressing a palm to her racing heart, she drew a breath. "Matteo. What-what are you doing here?"

Justin, his hand on the small of her back, stepped forward. "Man, she sent you the divorce papers."

Matteo clenched his jaw and narrowed his eyes at Justin. "I'm still her husband."

"Chloe?" Justin touched her arm, forcing her to meet his confused blue eyes.

"It's okay, Justin. You'd better leave. I'll call you later."

"You're sure?"

"Yes."

With a defiant glare at Matteo, Justin placed a tender kiss on Chloe's lips. Shoulders rigid, he headed toward the doorway where Matteo stood, a sentinel with arms folded across his broad chest.

In a display of testosterone, Matteo moved to allow Justin to brush by him, just barely. Justin's shoulder hit Matteo as he slipped out.

The outside door opened and closed, the sound signaling Chloe's showdown with her husband had come, in the way she'd feared it might.

Matteo's golden-brown eyes, framed by thick black lashes, met hers.

Her traitorous heart thumped. Unable to help herself, she scanned him. He'd gotten sexier, hotter, in the two years since she'd fled Italy. His black hair, worn a trifle too long, swept back from a face that could have been chiseled by Michelangelo. The sprinkling of gray hair at his temples and the fine lines of stress around his mouth gave him a vulnerability that increased his appeal. His narrow high-bridged nose flared slightly at the nostrils, betraying his agitation.

Chloe locked her knees and swallowed, willing strength into her spine. "Why *are* you here, Matteo? You didn't need to come in person to deliver the divorce papers."

He sauntered into the small room where she stored art pieces for her gallery, filling the space with the sheer power of his presence.

Unflinching, she stood her ground. "We haven't lived together for two years. I expect you to sign the papers. I know you received them. You haven't bothered to contact me in all this time, but here you are, barging in with that macho attitude that never worked on me."

"I hadn't expected to find you in the arms of another man and I reacted badly. I forget I have no say in what you do. I apologize."

His apology made her take a step back. The anger in his voice had cooled. The man standing before her, looking contrite, wasn't the same one she'd left.

"Who are you, and what have you done with Matteo?" she said.

"What?"

"A DiMarco apologizing. I never thought to see that. You've changed."

"Life has a way of doing that to a person."

Not wanting to dwell on the possible reasons for his change, she gathered her emotions around her like a protective shawl. "Why did you come all the way to Philadelphia?"

He moved closer until they were a whisper apart.

Regardless of the two years that passed, he made her want him again with a craving that threatened to overwhelm her senses. She clenched her hands at her sides, fighting the urge to run her fingers over the light stubble on his strong jaw, to ease the worry lines around his full, delectable lips.

"You need to come to Ravello with me," he said.

"Why?"

"Giuseppe is asking for you."

"How is your grandfather?"

"He's dying."

Chloe put a hand to her throat. "No, not Giuseppe. That wonderful man."

"He wants to see you before he—he goes."

"Of course. I'll book a flight and arrange for someone to look after things here. I'll be there for Giuseppe. I miss him."

"More than you miss me?" Matteo asked softly.

The thinly veiled pain in his eyes was almost her undoing. She reached out to touch his face, then pulled her hand away.

Matteo ran his fingers through his hair, mussing it and making him look adorably younger than his thirty-six years.

"My plane is ready to take us to Italy," he said. "We can't waste any time."

She shook her head. "I don't want to go with you. I'll book my own flight."

"Giuseppe needs us together. He said he'll die happy knowing you and I have reconciled."

"But we haven't."

Matteo's lips formed a wry smile. "I came to propose an arrangement."

Warning bells went off in her head. "Arrangement?"

"I know you love Grandfather and you want his last days to be peaceful. Come to Ravello with me. Convince him we've decided to give our marriage another chance. Then, I'll sign the papers."

Tension in every line of his body, he stared at her. "I need you to do this, Chloe. For Grandfather."

"You're blackmailing me."

He shrugged. "That's a harsh word. I only want to help my grandfather. Is it a deal?"

"I need to think about it. I don't like lying to him."

"I don't either, but I want him to die happy. He deserves that after all he's done for me."

She chewed her lip. "No matter what I decide, I want to see Giuseppe."

"Chloe, is everything alright?"

Chloe and Matteo turned to Janie, Chloe's assistant, who stood in the doorway, a hesitant expression on her face. "I'm sorry. He came in and asked where you were. I was busy with a customer and pointed to the storage room."

"It's okay. Janie, this is Matteo DiMarco."

"Matteo? *The* Matteo?" The middle-aged woman's eyes widened.

"Ciao, Janie. Yes, I am *the* Matteo, as you say." He turned to Chloe. "Unless you've got another Matteo around here."

"Nope." She couldn't handle one Matteo when she had him.

"It's-it's really nice to meet you," Janie said.

"Did you need anything?" Chloe asked the other woman, anxious to end the conversation before Janie blurted out something that would arouse Matteo's curiosity.

"Sadie Hunt's agent called about the showing next month. She says it's urgent and she has to talk to you."

"I'll call her right away. Thanks."

When they were alone again, Chloe turned to Matteo.

"As you can tell, this is my place of business. We can't talk here."

"It didn't look like you were conducting business with that Justin guy."

"What?"

"Forget it."

She decided to let his softly spoken comment about Justin go. "I'll meet you after I close. I'll give you my decision then."

"Tell me where you live, and I'll come to your place."

Panic and guilt coalesced into a tight ball in her chest. "That's not a good idea. My parents live with me."

"I like your parents. I'll stop by early and visit with them."

"No!" Anxiety made her voice squeak.

He frowned, marring his perfect features.

"Where are you staying?" she asked. "Maybe we can meet for drinks and we'll discuss things then."

He adjusted the cuffs on his snowy white dress shirt. The overhead light reflected on his cufflinks, bouncing golden sparks on the beige walls. "I'm staying at the Ritz-Carlton. I'll make reservations for dinner at the restaurant there. Seven o'clock work for you?"

She nodded, but before she could say another word, he'd walked out.

Her blood pumped loudly in her ears. She'd worked hard and carved out a good life for herself since she ran away from Italy, and Matteo. Despite urging from her parents and friends that Matteo deserved to know about the children, she'd kept quiet, out of fear and hurt. Now he was back, upsetting her well-ordered world, reviving dreams she'd left in Italy. And forcing the truth from her, one she should have told him years ago.

* * *

HER BAGS PACKED and waiting by her condo door, Chloe turned to the twin toddlers standing in front of her. She knelt, and they went into her arms.

"Joey, Sofie, you be good for Grandmom and Grandpop while I'm gone."

The twins nodded.

"They'll be fine," Chloe's mom said. "You take care of what you need to do in Italy and don't worry about us."

"I'll miss them." Chole grabbed the children to her, then kissed each sweet baby on the cheek. Holding their hands, she stood. "My car will be here soon. I need to stop by the gallery and talk to Janie before I head out to the airport."

"Please tell Matteo we send our hellos," her dad said.

"I will."

Her mother touched her arm. "You have to tell him about the children. You should have done it before now."

"I know, Mom. I was afraid, and the longer I put it off, the harder it's become. I'll wait until he's signed the divorce papers. I feel I'll have more leverage then, if needed. The DiMarco family is a powerful one in Italy."

"Isn't it cowardly to wait until he signs the papers?"

Chloe's phone, inside her purse, pinged, saving her from answering her mom. "That's probably my driver."

She bent to gather the twins into a fierce embrace. "I'll miss you both so much."

"Miss you, Mommy," they said in unison.

Chloe stood and hugged her parents. "I'll call as often as I can."

"Please do," her mom said. "We want to know how Giuseppe is doing. Please send him our good wishes."

Her heart heavy with anxiety, already missing her children, and apprehensive about what awaited her in Italy, Chloe went out to the car, her dad following with her suitcases.

Janie was closing the gallery when she arrived. "Busy day?" Chloe asked. "I wanted to be here, but packing and last-minute things took up my time. The last two days since Matteo showed up have been hectic."

"Charli and I handled everything."

"Are you sure you'll be okay running this place by yourself while I'm gone?"

"You've trained me well. It's not a problem, especially now that you took on help with Charli."

"Call me if you have any issues you can't resolve, any time of the day or night."

Janie laughed. "Go to Italy. We'll be fine. I'm sorry you're going because of that poor man's illness, but you get to spend time with hottie Matteo. You never mentioned how scorching he is."

Chloe rolled her eyes. "He and I will be divorced soon."

"I picked up vibes between you two the other day. I wouldn't be so sure about that divorce."

"Bite your tongue."

Laughing, the women hugged, and Chloe went out to the car, where the driver waited to open the door for her. She got in and clicked on her seatbelt. Shifting to make herself comfortable, she looked out the car window to the city rolling by in the gathering dusk, her mind replacing Philadelphia with the Amalfi Coast and Ravello.

CHAPTER 2

Matteo tossed back his drink. The whiskey slid smoothly down his throat, as only twenty-year-old Scotch could. He placed the empty glass on the table in front of him and settled into the leather seat in the cabin of his company's jet. Luciano, the flight attendant, brought him a fresh whiskey.

New drink in hand, Matteo sipped. The liquor refused to soothe him. His insides roiled like an untried boy waiting for his first date. Chloe would be here any minute for their flight to the small airport near Ravello.

Two days ago, he'd found her in the arms of another man. Since she'd left him, he'd sought out other women, trying to forget Chloe. He'd never allowed any of those women to get close. None compared to Chloe, the woman who'd captured his heart, then crushed it when she walked out on him without a word, leaving behind only a terse note and her engagement ring. The pain in his soul never left.

Knowing their marriage died a long time ago, he planned to sign the divorce papers when he received them, until Giuseppe revealed his illness. He'd come for Chloe only because of the elderly man they both loved.

Seeing her with another man revived the ache of her leaving, and the memories of how good they'd been together when they'd been so in love.

He finished his drink, seeking solace that never came.

The cockpit door was open, and Matteo could see the pilot and co-pilot going through the pre-flight preparations. They should take off in forty-five minutes. He heard voices, Luciano and a woman. Chloe. He'd never forgotten her throaty voice with its Philadelphia accent that became more pronounced when she was excited, especially when they made love. Images of her eagerness and willingness to experience all he could teach flooded him.

Chloe walked into the cabin, followed by Luciano pulling her suitcase. Dressed in stylish jeans that hugged her slim legs, and wearing a white silk blouse that stretched across her lush breasts, she stole his breath. Her brown hair grew past her shoulders, much longer than before. Coppery strands wove through her thick mane, replacing the blonde lights he remembered. She was all woman, sexy and confident.

She'd left him.

He'd let her go.

"Ciao, Chloe."

"Matteo."

"Did you get everything taken care of at the gallery?" he asked.

"Yes. Janie will handle things, with help from my friend Charli. The gallery is in good hands."

"Then, you can relax and put your mind at ease. Grandfather is our main concern now."

"I'll be there for Giuseppe, in every way." She threw her large black carry-on bag and her pale green purse onto one of the seats across the aisle, then sank into the seat next to them.

"Signora DiMarco, would you like something to eat or drink?" Luciano asked.

Chloe waved a hand toward Matteo's empty glass. "I'll have what he's having."

With a bow, the flight attendant went to the back of the cabin with her luggage.

Matteo raised an eyebrow. "Since when do you drink anything other than wine?"

"For a while now. My tastes have changed." Her unwavering gray eyes locked with his. "My taste in everything has changed."

Unwelcome anger and jealousy shot through him like a fiery ball. "Including men? You now go for the pale blond types?"

"Justin is a wonderful man, and a good friend. I won't discuss him with you."

"Do you love him?"

Surprise at his question lit her eyes.

Luciano arrived with their drinks. Chloe took hers, and ran a finger over the rim of her glass, as if lost in thought.

"You didn't answer my question, Chloe," Matteo said softly.

She raised her eyes to look into his. "I like Justin a lot."

Relief made Matteo's breath catch in his throat. He reached for his fresh drink and downed it.

Chloe smiled. "Aren't you supposed to sip that?"

He returned her smile. She didn't say she loved that other guy.

* * *

CHLOE OPENED her eyes and sat up, unsure where she was. She threw off her blanket and blinked to focus on her surroundings. The DiMarco corporate jet. She sank back into her seat.

"Sleep well?"

Matteo's words jerked her attention across the aisle.

He stared at her, his beautifully shaped lips tilted in a smile.

Her pulse double-timed at the intensity in his eyes. Whenever he looked at her, he'd always made her feel like she was the only person in the world, and he made her feel that way now.

"How long have I been out?" she asked, pushing aside thoughts that no longer had any place in her world.

"We land in forty-five minutes."

"I slept the whole flight?"

"You must have been very tired. You looked comfortable and I didn't want to disturb you, so I put a blanket over you and let you sleep."

"I never sleep on planes. I guess I wore myself out the

past few days getting ready for this trip." She stood and skimmed hands down the sides of her jeans.

Matteo's gaze followed the path of her hands.

She refused to acknowledge what she read in his darkened eyes. "I need to freshen up before we land."

He nodded toward her left hand. "I see you wear your wedding ring."

Not looking at him, she twisted the gold band on her finger. "I-I haven't worn it in a while, but if we're to convince your grandfather we've reconciled, I figured I should wear it."

Luciano came down the aisle, rolling a table holding a coffee carafe, mug, and a basket of assorted rolls, along with butter and jars of jam. He set the table in front of her, saving her from further conversation about the ring.

"Thanks, Luciano. Just what I need."

The plane touched down at a small private airstrip outside Ravello. When they alighted, Nunzio, the DiMarco driver, was waiting beside the black limo. His welcoming smile eased Chloe's jitters.

She strode to Nunzio and gave him a quick hug. Holding him at arms' length, she grinned. "Nunzio, it's good to see you again."

He touched the tip of his cap. "Good to see you again, Signora DiMarco."

Matteo walked up to them. "Plenty of time for reunions later. Could you please load our luggage into the car, Nunzio." Amusement tinted Matteo's voice.

"Of course, Signore DiMarco."

Chloe headed toward the limo. Unlike his mother,

Matteo found Chloe's friendliness toward the servants endearing and very American.

Matteo opened the back-passenger door, and she slid in. He climbed in after her.

Nunzio got in and put the car into gear. Soon they were heading along the Amalfi Coast to the DiMarco palazzo. Chloe relaxed into the luxurious seat and watched the airport and houses give way to the countryside and color-soaked magnificence of Amalfi.

Without speaking, she accepted a glass of champagne from Matteo. She'd come back to Italy for Giuseppe, the old man she loved like a grandfather. She hated lying to him about their marriage, but she wanted to make his last days happy. She didn't have to be anything more than cordial to Matteo when they were alone. Once she painted herself as a woman in love with her husband, she'd go back to Philadelphia, signed divorce papers in hand.

Guilt reared up. Before she left Italy again, she'd tell Matteo and Giuseppe the secret she'd carried for the past two years. Dread knotted her chest, anticipating Matteo's reaction to knowing they had two children together. She'd waited too long to tell him.

Intimidated by the noble and wealthy DiMarco's, and especially Matteo's royalty-obsessed mother Valentina, and upset Matteo dismissed her concerns about his mother's treatment of her, Chloe fled to Philadelphia and the loving arms of her family. Sure Matteo would follow, she planned to tell him about her pregnancy. When he didn't follow, or try to contact her, Chloe's heart broke.

She kept waiting for him to call, to tell her he loved her,

that he'd never been unfaithful, despite the stories about him and other women reported on the gossip sites. His silence communicated his feelings louder than words, and confirmed the stories about his infidelity were true. If he didn't love her, but he knew about her pregnancy, he'd want her to come back to him out of a sense of obligation. She wanted Matteo to want her for herself. Or so she rationalized.

She tilted her head to study him. His proud profile with his hawk-like nose and firm jaw spoke of a man used to getting what he wanted. He'd wanted her three years ago, and she'd given him her heart. Her craving for him had consumed her with a fire that had never extinguished. No man would ever again elicit that searing desire in her, and that was okay. She didn't want passion. She wanted stability.

Who are you kidding? a small voice said.

Forcing her mind from Matteo and images of making love with him, Chloe sat up to better take in the breathtaking scenery unfolding before them. The sun shone brightly in a cloudless cobalt sky. Far below them, the Mediterranean sparkled turquoise. Trees, their branches twisted by eons of wind, hugged the sides of the cliffs.

Nunzio took the hairpin turns of the Coast carefully. Memories of riding these same curves with Matteo in his Maserati scrolled through her mind like a colorful collage. She gripped the stem of her champagne flute. The first time she'd ridden with him, she'd white-knuckled the whole trip from Ravello to the DiMarco villa. Matteo liked to drive fast, but when he saw how scared she was, he'd slowed down. Still grieving her fiancé, who'd died three years before in a car accident, Chloe feared being in a fast car, especially over the narrow twists of the Amalfi Coast.

She shook aside thoughts of the past. She would focus on the here and now. "This is one of the most enchanted places on Earth."

"It will always be my home," Matteo said.

It had been her home once.

CHAPTER 3

The limo pulled up to the circular drive that fronted Villa DiMarco. Nunzio brought the car to a stop, jumped out, and opened the passenger door for Chloe. She exited slowly, then pivoted to take in the pearl-tinted stone and marble palazzo, gilded by the sun. As they had for decades, marble nymphs played in the fountain in the center of the drive. The soft tinkle of water lent musical serenity to the surroundings and comforted Chloe's worried heart.

She'd come home.

Matteo stood beside her and cupped her elbow. "Ready to do this?" he whispered in her ear.

Before she could answer, the heavy wooden front door opened and banged shut, shattering the peace. Matteo's mother Valentina, arms folded across her well-endowed chest, stood on the top step. Her blonde helmet-like hair didn't move in the strong breeze. Her dark eyes narrowed and she tapped her foot.

"*Quindi l'hai reportata indietro,*" Valentina spit out.

"*So, you have brought her back.*" Chloe knew enough Italian to translate Valentina's sharp words. "Hello, to you, too, Valentina." In the years since she left Italy, Chloe had grown stronger. Valentina no longer intimidated her.

"Speak English, Mama," Matteo said.

Valentina scanned Chloe with a look that could make grown men cry. Chloe stared back.

The older woman pulled the door open with a flourish and went back into the house, slamming the door behind her.

"Sorry about that," Matteo said.

The compassion in his voice surprised Chloe.

"Your mother hasn't changed her opinion of me."

"I told you years ago not to let her bother you," he said.

"She doesn't get to me, not any more. I can handle her."

"You're different, Chloe."

"In more ways than you know."

His hand on the small of her back, he led her into the house. "We've had a long flight and we're tired. The cook prepared a light meal which should be waiting in our suite. We rest today, and tomorrow we'll visit Giuseppe."

Chloe froze. "Wait. What? *Our* suite? I'm not sharing a room with you."

An exasperated sigh escaped him. "If we're to convince Grandfather we've reconciled, we must sleep in the same room."

She put a hand on her hip. "I get it. But not the same bed. Is that clear?"

"Perfectly."

* * *

RESTLESS AND WIDE AWAKE, unable to sleep on the uncomfortable chaise in their suite, and with the too-appealing Chloe nearby, Matteo sat on one of the palazzo's patios and sipped Campari. The slightly bitter taste of the aperitif matched his mood. The gentle lapping of the Mediterranean far below, its inky darkness broken by the golden path of the full moon, couldn't untangle his chaotic thoughts.

He'd made a mistake to bring Chloe here. Seeing her again, having her close, was an unwelcome reminder of all he'd lost that day she walked out. Chloe had hurt him, but he'd hurt her, too. Stubborn and proud, he'd thought only of himself.

He finished his drink and plunked the glass on the low table in front of him. Chloe had come back for his grandfather. They both loved the old man who'd raised Matteo, who occupied a special place in his heart. To make Giuseppe happy, he'd pay the price of being near Chloe and not touching her or making love with her.

She'd broken his heart.

He still wanted her.

CHAPTER 4

Sunlight teased Chloe's eyes open. She stretched like a contented cat. Fully awake, she remembered where she was and jolted up, clutching the bedsheets to her chest.

She twisted her head to the empty space beside her. Memories assaulted her. She slid her hand across the sheet to where Matteo had lain when they'd been happy and deliriously in love. In this bed, he'd opened her to the erotic delights of lovemaking and taught her how to please him—and satisfied her in ways she suspected no other man could.

Fighting to rein in her tortured thoughts, she scanned the luxurious suite. The bed faced two floor-to-ceiling windows that framed the turquoise waters of the Mediterranean below. A marble-topped table sat between the windows. On the table, replacing the daily vase of fresh flowers she remembered, a flat-screen TV stared at her, a mocking reminder of the changes in their lives. Too busy making love, she and Matteo had no time for TV in the bedroom.

The ivory walls matched the comforter on the bed. The floors were fawn-colored marble shot with black. Beige curtains trimmed in black fluttered in the flower-scented breeze. Other than the TV, the room remained unchanged.

Matteo had left everything the same.

She lay back on the pillow and pressed a palm to her fluttering heart. She wondered if he'd thought of her in the years separating them. She squeezed her eyes shut. He'd never called, never reached out, but she hadn't called him either. He'd come for her to help Giuseppe, nothing more.

When her racing heart settled, she sat up again. The bedside clock read nine. "Matteo!" she called out, to be sure he wasn't in the ensuite bathroom or his dressing room. Silence greeted her, along with a twinge of guilt. He'd slept on the satin chaise in the sitting area. Maybe she should allow him to sleep in the bed. Nervousness rippled through her. She couldn't trust herself so close to him.

A glimpse into the adjoining sitting room showed a small table set for breakfast with two chairs flanking it. Her stomach rumbled. She slipped out of bed, taking a moment to savor the smoothness of the cool marble on her bare feet.

She pressed the button on the wall to summon the maid with breakfast, then winced at how quickly old habits returned. She'd rather go to the kitchen and prepare her own meal, but she'd horrify the staff.

Breakfasted, showered, and dressed, Chloe strode toward the door when a soft knock stopped her.

"Chloe, are you dressed?" Matteo called from the other side.

She swallowed around the lump that formed in her throat. "You can come in, Matteo." Straightening her shoulders, she prepared to face him.

He stepped into the room, triggering Chloe's pulse up a few notches. No fair he looked so scrumptious and sexy, especially in the morning. She filled her ravenous gaze with him. Black tailored pants, custom-made no doubt, showcased legs that went on forever. On his feet, he wore black loafers without socks. His white shirt was untucked and stretched over a muscled chest she recalled too well. A lock of dark hair fell over his forehead. The glint in his eyes told her he knew she checked him out, and he liked it.

His eyes trailed over her. "You look good."

"Thanks." Stifling the pleasure of his compliment, she looked away. Truth be told, she'd dressed with care for him, pairing pale pink silk Capris with a white silk top. Her pink kitten-heeled sandals matched her Capris.

"I like your hair long," he said, his voice husky. "I like the red highlights, too."

Edginess made her skim a hand over her hair. Wanting to appear professional, she usually wore it pinned up when in the gallery. In Italy all those years ago, she'd lost her inhibitions. She sensed her hang-ups slipping away again.

"Ready for my grandfather?" Matteo asked.

"I can't wait to see him. I only wish it were under better circumstances."

They walked down the long hallway to Giuseppe's quarters. Her heels clacked on the polished pale green marble speckled with white, the sound ramping up her anxiety. Her insides shook, and she ran her hands down the sides of her pants. She would put on a good front for Giuseppe.

A woman dressed in nurse's scrubs opened the door at Matteo's knock. She ushered them in, then closed the door.

"Il signor DiMarco si sente bene oggi e non vede l'ora della tua visita."

"Mr. DiMarco is feeling well today and looking forward to your visit," Chloe translated in her head. She smiled at the nurse. "Grazie."

The woman gestured toward the suite's patio that overlooked the Amalfi Coast.

Matteo held Chloe's elbow as they strolled to where his grandfather waited.

The gentle pallet of turquoise and white that dominated the rooms brought the sea indoors and gave the space the sensation of floating lazily on the water. Chloe had always loved these rooms.

Giuseppe came into view, and Chloe gasped. The stooped figure sitting in a wheelchair, a white shawl around his shoulders, bore little resemblance to the vibrant elderly man Chloe knew. He turned at their approach.

She steeled herself to smile, hiding her dismay.

His light brown eyes, so like Matteo's, lit when he saw her. He held out a hand, blue veins showing starkly against his transparent skin. "Chloe, my dear, come here."

He spoke in English, melting her heart, rather than have her struggle through Italian.

She braced herself against the feebleness in his voice. Forcing her legs to move, she went to him and knelt to hug him. She fought tears at his thinness and his parchment-like skin.

Giuseppe wrapped his arms around her with a strength she wouldn't have suspected. Finally, he freed her, his keen eyes studying her. "You want to cry, child. Don't weep for me. I've had a good life, a full life. Soon, I'll join my beloved Sofia."

Chloe sat in a chair next to him and reached out to clutch both his hands in hers. "Giuseppe, don't talk like that. You must have hope. You must fight. We don't want to lose you."

"My dear, the decision is not yours or mine." He chuckled. "Enough about me. You look well. You've matured since you were here. I notice a new confidence in you. That is good."

He looked over at Matteo, lounging by the doorway. "Come, son, join us."

In an effort to tame her riotous emotions, Chloe took deep breaths and focused on the colorful vegetation spread before her like a still life painting by a master.

Matteo sat on the other side of Giuseppe. Giuseppe released his hands from Chloe and grabbed one of Matteo's, joining Chloe and Matteo's hands. Hers looked small and pale, enveloped in Matteo's large, strong, tanned ones.

Matteo's warm flesh heated Chloe with remembrances of the love they'd shared, of their short-lived happiness.

Sadness for what might have been threatened to overpower her. With effort, she pushed the sorrow away.

"Seeing you together has made this old man happy," Giuseppe said. "You belong with each other. Selfish, conniving people drove you apart. And you failed to have faith in each other. Promise me you won't let that happen again."

His soft eyes looked from one to the other.

Guilt gnawed at Chloe. She loved Giuseppe and hated lying to him. She'd come all this way to make him happy.

"I promise, Giuseppe." She resisted the urge to cross the fingers of her free hand behind her back.

With an expectant expression, Giuseppe turned to Matteo.

Matteo drew an audible breath and looked at her, then back to his grandfather. "I promise also, Grandfather."

The old man's weathered, sun-browned face broke out in a bright smile. "Good, good. Now, we celebrate with some of the finest wine from our vineyards."

CHAPTER 5

Their visit with Giuseppe exhausted the old man, and his nurse insisted he rest. Promising to stop by later, Chloe and Matteo left.

Outside the room, Matteo turned to her. "I must attend to work. Will you be all right by yourself?"

"Of course. I want to walk around the property and visit with the servants."

Smiling, he shook his head. "You drove Mama crazy with your friendliness toward our staff. That is not done in her world."

Chloe laughed. "I knew it drove her crazy, and I liked it. I'll like it more now that she's living here."

A huge grin split his face. "I think Mama is in for a shock."

His eyes darkened and his features sobered. He reached out a hand to tuck strands of her hair behind her ear. His long, slim fingers provoked regret and yearning within her.

"You are more beautiful than I remember, Chloe," he said, his voice rough. "It wasn't all bad between us, was it?"

Words stuck in her throat.

"Does this Justin make you feel the way I did? Does he make you passionate and hungry for him, as you were with me?" His eyes and words told her he still desired her.

Her traitorous body responded, swaying toward him.

Reality reared up, and she stepped back, away from temptation she didn't think she could resist.

"What is between Justin and me is none of your business."

"You are still my wife."

"Not for long," she shot back.

Hurt flashed in his eyes before a mask settled over his features. He turned on his heel and stalked away.

The thump of his shoes on the marble echoed the pounding of her heart.

* * *

"What did you say?" Matteo looked up from his papers to his secretary seated in front of his desk in the villa's office.

"Would that be all?" Nico asked.

Matteo waved a hand in dismissal. "Yes. Type up your notes and email them to me before you leave for the day."

"Very good."

Once Nico left, Matteo settled back in his chair. He'd had a hard time concentrating on business. Chloe dominated his thoughts. He shouldn't have brought her here he told himself for the hundredth time. He did it for his grandfather.

He'd acted like a jerk with her earlier today. They hadn't lived together in two years. Their divorce would be final not long after he signed the papers. He grabbed the silver pen off his desk and threw it across the room. The action did nothing to vent his frustration. Chloe had every right to her own life. Even so, the thought of her with another man painted a picture in his head he didn't want to see, and he'd lashed out by reminding her of her passion for him. He was an arrogant ass.

"Signore DiMarco."

Matteo looked toward the doorway to the butler standing there.

"What is it, Federico?"

"We have a dinner guest tonight."

The beginnings of a headache pounded Matteo. He knew what was coming. "Who is it?"

"Your uncle's widow."

Federico's face revealed nothing of his feelings, but Matteo knew only Valentina could tolerate Ingrid. He couldn't understand why his mother held such friendliness to her brother-in-law's widow. He suspected they were like matching statues, sculpted by the same artist, where wealth and social standing meant everything.

His mother arranged Ingrid's visit to make Chloe uncomfortable. He hoped Chloe had the backbone now to handle both women at the same time. Husbandless and broke, Ingrid had let Matteo know she wanted to rekindle their long-ago affair. He'd met the beautiful blonde bombshell at university where she was an exchange student from

Sweden. Sexy and seductive, most of the men, and half the women, wanted Ingrid. He'd won her. In love for the first time, he brought her home to meet his family. When she met his Uncle Santino, she'd pursued the much older, much richer man, with the tenacity of a lion on the hunt.

Valentina and Ingrid had driven the final wedge between him and Chloe.

He would never forgive them. Or himself for not fighting for his wife.

Federico cleared his throat, letting Matteo know he was still there, waiting.

"Thank you, Federico. Alert the cook."

"As you say, signore."

The butler left as quietly as he'd come. Matteo rubbed a hand over his eyes as scenes from the past, like videos on fast forward, flashed across his mind.

He'd gotten over Ingrid's betrayal and met Chloe, a woman he loved in ways he never did Ingrid. Then, he lost Chloe. She hadn't trusted him enough to ignore the rumors planted by Ingrid and his mother, and the phony stories in the gossip rags and online sites. Despite his marriage, the magazines had continued to publish bogus articles and pictures that had him seducing supermodels and princesses. He should have realized how hard it had been for Chloe to hear the rumors and see the photos. His own stubbornness and pride prevented him from understanding her hurt. Or going after her when she left.

"Enough!" he said to the empty room. He would not revisit the past.

* * *

CHLOE SAT at a table on one of the patios and sipped the delicate white wine she'd enjoyed with a light lunch of roasted chicken and grilled vegetables. Here at the villa, she was surrounded by an abundance of colors and lush beauty everywhere she looked. Her condo in Philadelphia had only a small balcony with a view of the building across the way.

A maid bustled in to clear the dishes. Chloe smiled at her. "Grazie, Teresa."

The young woman smiled shyly and curtsied.

When Chloe lived here as Matteo's wife, the maids had a habit of curtsying to the family. No matter how many times she asked them not to, they kept doing it. She suspected Valentina, with her obsession with royalty, had drummed it into the maids to curtsy to the family members.

Sighing, Chloe looked out to the gardens. Flowers in an artist's palette of bright colors hugged the cliffside, creating a flamboyant trail to the indigo sea below. A small tree, twisted by the winds through the eons, stretched toward the water, like a figure grasping for something just out of reach. She'd painted that scene when she'd lived here as Matteo's wife. The painting now resided in a closet in her Philadelphia condo. To look at it reminded her of all she and Matteo had shared, and all they'd lost.

She set her empty glass on the table and stood. No more thinking of the past with its regrets. A pleasant, soothing walk in the gardens would relax her.

Inhaling the sweet scent of flowers, she went down the marble steps to the cobblestone path that wound through the extensive shrubbery and flowers. No gardeners worked today. Peace enveloped her. Seabirds squawked overhead, and the soft breeze rustled the leaves of the trees. The flowering shrubs that lined the paths brushed her, soft as a painter's touch, as she passed.

Ahead, under the leafy branches of an Italian Cypress, she spotted the stone bench next to a marble statue of the Roman god Bacchus holding up a goblet of wine. Matteo had kissed her for the first time as they sat on that bench. She skimmed a finger over her lips, feeling again his lips coaxing, teasing, urging her to give more. She'd returned his kiss with all the hunger he incited in her.

Blowing out a breath, she forced herself to walk to the bench and sit. She would not allow the past to dictate her future. The gentle lap of the sea far below lulled her into serenity. Closing her eyes, she concentrated on the music of birds twittering in the branches, the perfume of the flowers, the shrill call of seabirds.

Ravello was a magical place made for love. In the years since she'd fled the cruelty of Valentina and Ingrid and the never-ending gossip about Matteo and other women, she'd missed the sensuality of Ravello.

She'd missed Matteo.

CHAPTER 6

Chloe put on her gold hoop earrings, the only jewelry she would wear tonight, other than the gold band that had been her wedding ring. She'd taken it off the day she left Matteo, and until now, it had resided at the bottom of her jewelry box. She touched her neckline, remembering the silver necklace with the flower motif pendant she bought the day she met Matteo. She hadn't worn it the past two years. For a reason she couldn't explain, she packed the necklace for this trip back to Italy.

She studied herself in the mirror. Dressed for dinner in an elegant beige silk sheath and wearing sky-high matching sandals, she looked every bit the wealthy Italian socialite. She wrinkled her nose and turned away. She was no longer that woman, if indeed she ever was. She would play the part for Giuseppe, who would join them tonight.

If she were honest with herself, she also wanted to show up their dinner guest, Ingrid. Anxiety and anger coalesced in her chest, and she drew shallow breaths. Unlike before, she would not let Ingrid bully her.

Matteo, adjusting the cuffs on his white dress shirt, stepped out of his dressing room. He reached for his jacket draped over a chair and stopped. Their gazes met. The golden flecks in his eyes sparked. His slow, sensual scan of her body provoked heat in her and a longing for what only he could give her, for what they'd once shared.

"Beautiful," he whispered.

Chloe's pulse spiked as she performed a leisurely scan of his body. Despite his businesslike attire of white shirt and gray suit pants, animal magnetism throbbed from him. His gray and mauve tie perfectly complemented the suit. His dark hair was slicked back from his chiseled face.

Magnifico. The Italian word for magnificent popped into her mind.

She glared at him, using anger to hide her pleasure at his compliment and the desire for him that swept her. "When were you going to tell me Ingrid will be at dinner tonight?"

He released a frustrated sigh, slipped on his jacket, and adjusted his cuffs. "I found out this afternoon. I would have told you before dinner." He frowned. "How did you know?"

"I went to the kitchens to say hello to Lucia. I had to hear about our guest from the cook because my *husband* didn't think I needed that information."

He moved closer and cupped her shoulders. "I'm sorry. I should have let you know earlier so you could prepare yourself."

"I will not play her game a second time. I never could

figure out why she chose to go after me. You and she had broken up before we ever met, and she was married to your uncle. So why try to come between us?"

"I suspect it has something to do with Ingrid's ego. She always had men groveling at her feet. After she and Uncle Santino married, she tried to seduce me. When she saw how in love with you I was, she knew I'd never succumb to her." He shook his head. "She's not important and I don't care what she does so long as she doesn't hurt you. Let's not talk of her again."

He moved back. "I don't want to see my uncle's widow any more than you do. We'll put up a united front and handle her and Mama."

Refusing to soften, despite the warmth she felt that Matteo didn't want her hurt, Chloe raised her chin. "The united front we didn't put up before."

His features tensed. "We both made mistakes." He took her left hand and raised it to his lips to kiss her wedding band. "Leave the past behind tonight."

MATTEO USUALLY LOVED the cook's exquisite ravioli with puttanesca sauce, but tonight everything tasted like sawdust. He grabbed his glass of pinot noir and took a large sip. Nothing could wash away his distaste of sitting at the dining room table with Ingrid.

A balmy sea-scented breeze blew through the expansive room from the French doors opened to the balcony. Outside, darkness had settled and the night insects had started their lovely symphony.

Inside, tension was an uninvited guest at the table.

His mother signaled to Federico, who came quickly over.

"Si, Signora DiMarco."

"Tell Lucia her sauce didn't contain enough spice. I am not happy."

Federico bowed. "I will tell her."

Giuseppe, seated across from Valentina, plunked his glass down. The wine swirled in the glass, then settled.

"The sauce is perfect as always," he said in English. "I told you to speak English in front of Chloe."

"*Il mio Italiano 'e migliorato*," Chloe said. "Which is why I understood what Valentina said."

Matteo hid his smile with another sip of wine. Chloe's Italian *had* improved. No doubt she'd taken lessons since she left two years ago. He wondered why she felt it necessary to improve her Italian if she no longer lived with him. That was a question for another day.

Chloe, sitting at the other end of the table, smiled at him. He held up his glass to her in salute.

"My Italian is perfect," Ingrid said in English, her Swedish accent thick. All attention turned to her. She lifted her shoulders, bared by the thin straps of her form-fitting dress. "I speak six languages, all well."

"No need to remind us of how wonderful you are, Ingrid," Chloe said, amusement in her voice.

Matteo threw back his head and laughed. Chloe wasn't the shy woman he'd married three years ago. He liked the new Chloe even better than the old one.

He exchanged more smiles with her. Pleased that her

animosity toward him seemed to abate tonight, he reminded himself she played a part for the others.

The maids served the main course, grilled salmon and vegetables. The group talked of inconsequential subjects, thankfully in English.

The rigid set of his mother's shoulders told Matteo her coolness toward Chloe hadn't subsided. He loved his mother, but her obsession with royalty and family name had driven a spike into his marriage. Too proud, too self-absorbed, he hadn't realized what was happening until it was too late. That Chloe hadn't had enough faith in him wounded his ego and his heart.

It was too late now to make things right with his soon-to-be-ex-wife. He speared a piece of fish and slipped it into his mouth, chewing slowly as if he could shred the sadness that pierced him.

Although she spoke little during the meal, Ingrid sent cutting glances toward Chloe. Chloe paid her no attention. Pride for Chloe's grace swelled in Matteo, but his stomach churned. Chloe's calmness reinforced she cared nothing for him now.

He reached for his wine as an antidote to the surprising pain that thought invoked.

Sipping his drink, a delightful sauvignon blanc, he watched Chloe. She was deep in conversation with Giuseppe. When she laughed at something his grandfather said, Matteo's heart jumped. Chloe was beautiful, inside and out. Her large transparent gray eyes shone with kindness and intelligence. He gripped the stem of his glass. He wanted her again, craved her responsive body under his, her passionate kisses, her willingness to do whatever he desired in bed.

He wanted her love. The surprising and jolting admission made him gulp the rest of his drink, eliciting a disapproving cluck of her tongue from his mother.

The tense dinner over, the group prepared to move to the patio for espresso and dessert. Matteo started toward Chloe, but Ingrid, hips swaying, sauntered up to him. She ran her hand over his arm and stared up at him. Her blue eyes lit with an invitation, one he'd refused time and again.

"You get hotter every time I see you, Matteo," she purred.

Ignoring her comment, he said, "Let's join the others."

He stepped away. She slipped her arm through his, pressing close.

His mouth in a thin line, he had no choice but to escort her outside. Santino's will had given most of his extensive estate to his children, and provided a generous annual stipend to the wife he'd thrown over for Ingrid. He'd left Ingrid an apartment in Ravello and a small amount of money she'd blown in the six months since she'd been widowed.

On the hunt for another wealthy benefactor, Ingrid proved dangerous.

CHAPTER 7

Chloe sat next to Giuseppe at the glass-topped table. Valentina and Ingrid, across from them on the balcony, huddled in conversation. Chloe ignored the women as she'd done at dinner.

The women drew apart, and Valentina smiled at Chloe. Her smile didn't reach her eyes, but Chloe gave her points for trying to be friendly.

"You look very nice tonight, Chloe," Valentina said.

Momentarily taken aback, Chloe couldn't speak. "Thank you," she finally managed.

Valentina's surprising friendliness didn't ring true. Chloe chided herself on being too suspicious. Maybe the woman had had a change of heart toward her. Or maybe Matteo's mother tried to cover up that she and Ingrid had been gossiping about Chloe.

She glanced to Matteo seated at the other end of the table. He stared out over the water of the Mediterranean below, a pensive expression on his face. Chloe wondered what he was thinking, if he thought of her and all they'd once meant to each other. Remembrances of the past had been her constant companion since Matteo suddenly showed up in her gallery.

"I am very glad you are here, Chloe." Giuseppe interrupted her musings. "You make my grandson happy."

"It is no secret you are not the woman I would have chosen for my son, but I see how much happier he is when you are here." Valentina spoke slowly as if she had difficulty getting the words out.

Chloe widened her eyes. Things were getting way too surreal. Valentina saying nice things to her? She must have entered a parallel universe.

"Thank you, Valentina, I think."

Matteo chuckled. "Mama, you never cease to amaze."

His mother shrugged and picked up her cup of espresso. "I am only stating what I have noticed with my own eyes."

With a huff, Ingrid got up and left the table.

Some of the tension left with Ingrid. Chloe smiled at Giuseppe. "I wish our reunion were under better circumstances."

He waved a hand. "It is as it should be. I will die a contented man, knowing you and Matteo are together, where you belong."

Guilt constricted her chest.

Chloe felt someone watching and turned to find Matteo's penetrating gaze on her. Longing flared deep inside her. At one time he'd belonged to her. She grabbed her espresso and drank it in one swallow. It burned a trail down her throat, but couldn't extinguish her still-smoldering desire for her husband. Federico hurried over to refill her cup.

"Giuseppe." Valentina's voice disturbed the quiet and made the others turn to her. "I have invited Ingrid to stay with us for a while. She is all alone in that small apartment in Ravello."

Giuseppe visibly stiffened. "Valentina, this is my home. Perhaps you should have consulted with me before you invited Ingrid."

Valentina's heavily made-up eyes registered surprise. "Giuseppe, you wouldn't turn a family member into the street. Ingrid is lonely."

"She has a place to live," he said. "If it's not to her liking, perhaps she should get a job and buy a bigger apartment."

"Mama, Ingrid creates chaos wherever she goes. You should have talked to Grandfather and me before you invited her," Matteo said.

Valentina lifted her shoulders. "Ingrid is a DiMarco, after all."

No one spoke.

Giuseppe set down his empty cup. "I am tired."

Matteo stood. "Come, Grandfather, Chloe and I will take you to your room."

With Giuseppe between them, and each holding one of his elbows, Chloe and Matteo escorted the elderly man to his suite.

At the door, he turned to Chloe. "I hope Valentina and Ingrid together here won't make life difficult for you."

"Don't worry about it, Giuseppe. I'm not."

His nurse was waiting, and took charge of Giuseppe when they entered his quarters.

"Grandfather, you need to rest. Chloe and I need a peaceful walk in the gardens." Matteo touched her arm. "Okay with you?"

"I would love a walk in the gardens."

Giuseppe's smile lit his face and erased all remnants of his sickness. "Please, enjoy yourself with your wife."

Matteo took her hand and held onto it as they headed outside. Chloe knew she should free herself, but the warmth of his flesh on hers filled her with the tranquility she needed. They wandered down the steps leading to the gardens. She inhaled the sweet scents of flowers. Night birds and insects serenaded them as they followed the cobblestone trail. Days after arriving at the palazzo three years ago, she and Matteo had walked this same path. He'd excited her then like no other man ever had. He still had that effect on her.

Reality, like a sculptor's chisel, cut into her thoughts. Those times were gone forever. She released her hand from his. He let her go, then stopped. They faced each other.

"Why do you pull away, Chloe?"

"We agreed to put on our act in front of the others. No one else is around."

"Maybe I want to touch you," he said softly.

"You shouldn't." She couldn't admit she craved his closeness.

"I'm sorry Mama invited Ingrid to stay. I don't want you to feel uncomfortable. I will have a talk with Mama."

"Let it go. I can handle them. Your mother's left-handed compliment to me was a surprise. Maybe she's softened toward me."

"Or, as she said, she realizes you make me happy."

"Let's not go there. I don't have a problem with your mother and Ingrid together. I won't be here long anyway."

"Are you that anxious to escape me again?"

Not knowing how to answer, she rubbed her arms and focused on the dark waters below.

"Chloe," he whispered, his voice low and thick with emotion.

He gripped her shoulders and turned her to face him. His eyes were dark and mysterious in the pale moonlight. He caressed her cheek with his thumb. Her body tingled and she swayed toward him. His lips brushed hers, his touch whisper-soft. Her mind screamed to resist, but her heart refused to listen. His soft lips enticed and teased. She molded her body to his and wound her arms around his neck.

Parting her lips, she invited his possession. His tongue filled her mouth, exploring. With a low murmur, he gathered her closer and palmed her nape. She uttered whimpers she barely recognized as her own. Her insides flipped and begged for more. He left her mouth to trail hot kisses down her throat to her collarbone, then slid his hands along her ribcage to her hips. Holding her hips, he pressed her closer. She felt his hard erection against her stomach. Throwing her head back, she gave herself over to his sensual ministrations.

The squawk of a seabird penetrated her sexual haze. Her sanity returned. She pushed away from him and immediately wanted his intimacy again.

"We can't do that," she said in a trembling voice.

He touched her chin with his fingers until she met his dark gaze. "We desire each other and we always will."

She straightened her clothes. "That can't happen again."

"It will, Chloe, because we both want it."

* * *

AFTER A RESTLESS NIGHT populated by erotic dreams of Matteo, Chloe woke to bright sunlight and a quiet suite. She looked at the clock and threw off the bedcovers of fine Egyptian cotton sheets and silk comforter. In less than an hour, she had to be at Giuseppe's apartments to read to him.

She wondered where Matteo was. What he did no longer concerned her. She would leave here, signed divorce papers in hand, and Matteo would be out of her life for good. Just what she wanted. The kiss they'd shared last night painted a different picture. He still made her melt with a look, a touch.

Get real, she told herself. Matteo would never be completely out of her life, not when she confessed the secret she'd kept these past two years. Any desire he still felt for her would evaporate when he discovered he had two children she held from him. Maybe when she explained why she'd made the choice she did, he'd understand and not hate her.

She clutched the bed covers in her hand. She didn't want him to hate her.

"Stop!" she said to the empty room. Determined to

force him, that kiss, and her guilt-edged worry out of her mind, she stomped to the bathroom.

After showering, she pulled together a comfortable casual look of tan Capris, gray tank top, and tan Espadrilles. In the main kitchen, Lucia greeted her with a smile and gestured for her to sit at the large wooden table while she fixed Chloe breakfast. Chloe elected to take her breakfast in the homey kitchen rather than the lonely suite. Her meal over, she headed to Giuseppe's quarters, feeling more lighthearted than she had in a while.

The elderly man waited for her on his patio. He sat in his wheelchair, a blanket of vivid blues and greens across his knees.

"Grandfather." She leaned in to kiss his cheek, then settled into the chair next to him and picked up a book from the table between them.

"Is this what you want me to read to you?" The book was part of a mystery series set in Ancient Rome with a Roman senator as the protagonist and detective. "You remembered how much I love this series."

"Of course. Our times reading the antics of the crime-solving youthful Roman senator are some of the fondest of my life."

"Thank you for providing the English version."

He laughed. "I won't make you struggle through the Italian."

"I appreciate that, even though my Italian is better." Chloe opened the book to the first page, preparing to read.

Giuseppe put his hand on her arm, stopping her.

Frowning, she looked up at him.

"I am proud of you, Chloe. I understand your gallery in Philadelphia is quite successful."

"Thanks to you and the artists and patrons you sent my way."

He smiled. "It was the least I could do. I would have lent you any money you needed, but I knew you would not ask for help."

"You know me well, Giuseppe."

His sparkling brown eyes grew serious. "My dear, my grandson has been miserable since you left, short-tempered, yelling at staff. Not at all himself." He grinned. "Even Valentina sees how happy you make him."

Old hurts surfaced in Chloe. "I would think he could find a model or a princess to take my place." Her face heated, and she put a hand to her throat. "I'm sorry. That was so catty and mean."

"I am not offended, but that is behind you now. You are here, where you belong, with Matteo." Giuseppe studied her. "I think you have grown and are stronger now. So is my grandson."

"Thank you."

"Matteo has devoted the past two years to building our company and increasing our fortune, leaving him little time for much else."

"I didn't know that."

"The pressure on him has been even more tremendous since Santino died, leaving Matteo to run the entire organization by himself. I worry about him. Now that you are here again, perhaps he can learn to relax. You must both ignore the women who conspired against you before and forget the rumors in the magazines. Those magazines print what they think will sell. You and Matteo didn't trust each other enough to fight the viciousness. It is different now."

Chloe slid her gaze from his. He had such hope for her and Matteo. She prayed he never learned the truth about their marriage.

CHAPTER 8

Matteo's body ached from another uncomfortable night on the chaise. He'd gotten up early and dressed for the day. His business over for the morning, he pushed away from his desk and massaged his temple where the beginnings of a headache pulsed. The kiss he and Chloe shared last night dominated his thoughts and his dreams, making it hard to focus on work. He'd never stopped wanting her, doubted he ever would. As his American friends would say, he was screwed.

He and Chloe had agreed to lunch together. He went in search and found her in his grandfather's suite. Matteo stood in the doorway and drank in the sight of her leaning over his grandfather, who slept in his wheelchair. She adjusted the blanket around the old man's knees and kissed him on the cheek. Even with little makeup, her thick hair pulled into a high ponytail, and wearing casual clothes, she was the sexiest woman he'd ever known.

The love and tender care she showed his grandfather

touched him and tore a small hole in the protective wall he'd built around his heart.

Chloe straightened and glanced up. Surprise flashed across her face when she saw him. She put a finger to her lips, signaling quiet. She walked silently toward him, and he moved into the hall, with her close behind. Her jasmine scent provoked images of holding her, of lazy days spent in bed, talking, confessing his dreams and aspirations, of her understanding him as no one could. He needed her love, her kindness, in his life again. Those days were gone.

"How was he?" he asked, unsuccessfully fighting his regret at what he could never again have.

"Good, but he tires easily."

Giuseppe's nurse came down the hall and nodded to them.

"He's napping," Chloe told the nurse in Italian.

"You surprise me with your Italian," Matteo said. "Even your accent is good."

"Of course. What did you expect?"

"I'm not sure. Let's not talk of that now. Lunch is ready. After we eat, I'll take you to the gallery. Francesca is anxious to see you. They're closed today so you and she can have an uninterrupted visit."

LUNCH OVER, they headed toward the Sofia DiMarco Gallery on the expansive property. Something else would occupy Chloe's mind besides the infuriating and so-appealing man beside her.

Excitement rose in her as they neared the modern one-story stucco building housing the exhibit, which contained artwork—paintings, sculpture, ceramics, Murano glassware—Matteo's grandmother collected in her travels around the world with Giuseppe. A separate driveway led from the street to the building, with a small visitors parking lot.

Matteo opened the door for Chloe and stood back to let her enter. She inhaled the perfumed scent from vases of fresh-cut flowers strategically arranged around the large, open space. She'd started the practice of using fresh flowers. She smiled, pleased Francesca, the new director, had continued the tradition. When Chloe left two years before, she'd written a lengthy note to Giuseppe thanking him for the opportunity of managing the gallery and suggesting Francesca as the new director. She was happy Giuseppe had concurred about Francesca.

The light wood floors gleamed in the sunlight streaming through the Palladian windows. The sunbeams highlighted the museum's central piece, a large blue Murano vase Sofia had bought in Venice on her and Giuseppe's honeymoon.

At the back of the room Chloe glimpsed the souvenir shop, an idea she'd come up with. The gallery charged a small entrance fee. Money from the fee and the souvenir shop went to a home for orphaned and at-risk children and a cat sanctuary in Ravello, two of Sofia's favorite charities.

"Chloe!" Francesca, her dark hair flying around her face, came into the room from the offices in the rear. Arms outstretched, she ran to Chloe.

Laughing, the women embraced. Chloe held Francesca at arms' length and studied her. The young woman had matured since the days she'd been Chloe's assistant, working with her to set up the displays. A new confidence lit her olive-skinned face, and her brown eyes sparkled.

"You look great," Chloe said. "And so does this place. You've done a wonderful job."

"I had a good teacher," Francesca said with her musical accent. "You are more beautiful than ever." She looked over at Matteo and smiled. "I am so happy you are together. I always knew Chloe would come back."

Guilt hit Chloe like paint thrown in her face. Not only were Matteo and she deceiving Giuseppe, but also loyal Francesca, who'd been her only friend, other than Matteo and his grandfather.

"Tell me what's been happening in your life, then you must take me on a tour." Chloe scanned the room. Images, like colorful photos, zoomed through her mind. She'd spent the happiest days of her life here, handling the exquisite artifacts, falling in love with Matteo. She longed for those days.

To divert her mind from memories that had no place in her life now, Chloe slipped her arm through Francesca's. "Let's have coffee and talk. Are you still with that terrific guy Tommaso?"

Francesca's trilling laugh filled the room as they walked. "Tommaso and I married last year."

Chloe stopped and hugged Francesca. "That's wonderful."

With a shy smile, the young woman said, "We hope to start a family soon."

Her words provoked a fresh round of angst to rip through Chloe.

She and Matteo had a family, one he didn't know about.

The women continued their stroll to the employee break room in the back of the gallery. Chloe twisted her head to look back at Matteo.

He regarded them with a wistful expression.

She waved at him. "Matteo, join us."

His features softening, he followed them.

CHAPTER 9

Chloe promised Francesca she'd come back the next day to help her when the gallery was open to visitors. She loved being surrounded by the beauty of the objects Sofia DiMarco had collected.

As she left the gallery with Matteo, he received a call he said he had to take. He headed to his office while Chloe went to their room.

With free time, she called her parents. "Hi, Mom," she said when her mother answered. After exchanging pleasantries, Chloe sat on the edge of the bed. "How are they?" Hearing the children napped, disappointment tugged her. "Don't wake them. I'd hoped to talk to them, but maybe next time. How are things going?"

She and her mom spoke another fifteen minutes. With a sigh, Chloe disconnected the call. She missed home and the twins. Yet, she had to be here for Giuseppe. Her thoughts heavy, she trudged to the sitting room and sank onto the chaise. She had to tell Matteo about the children. And soon. He deserved to know.

Her pregnancy had been her salvation during the dark days following the end of their marriage. Her hope Matteo would follow her to Philadelphia had died with each passing day when she heard nothing from him. The twins, Giuseppe and Sofia, called Joey and Sofie by Chloe and her family, filled the empty places in her heart.

Drawing deep breaths to release the ball of anxiety that tightened in her chest, her mind traveled back two years, before she left Italy and Matteo. Forlorn without Matteo, who was on a business trip to Paris, Chloe flew there to surprise him and tell him the news of her pregnancy. She found his hotel room door unlocked and a naked Ingrid in his bed. Matteo wasn't in the room, and Ingrid said he'd asked her to wait for him while he attended meetings. Chloe had returned immediately to Italy.

He'd called her several times after that, but Chloe wouldn't take the calls. Upset and seething with anger, her heart broken, she had to discuss evidence of his infidelity to his face, and not in a phone call.

Days later, still reeling from his betrayal, Chloe entered the villa after a day at the gallery and heard voices on one of the first-floor patios. She headed there to investigate. Valentina, staying at the palazzo for a few weeks while her apartment was undergoing renovations, sat with a friend. Wine and a tray of antipasto were on the table before them. They didn't see Chloe, and she started to walk away when she heard her name. She knew just enough Italian to make out the gist of the women's conversation, one that sent her fleeing to her room. Leaning against the closed door, she knew she couldn't stay there and deal with Matteo's family any longer, not with a baby on the way. She feared what Valentina would do once she found out about the pregnancy.

A soft knock on the door brought Chloe back to the present. "Come in."

Matteo entered, holding his phone, his face glum.

She jumped up from the chaise and strode into the bedroom. "What's wrong?"

"Problem at our distribution center in Paris. I have to leave right away. I might be gone several days."

The mention of Paris ratcheted up Chloe's pulse. They stared at each other, and she knew he, too, remembered Paris, and its role in the demise of their tension-filled marriage. Although Matteo had insisted he had nothing to do with Ingrid being in his bed, Chloe hadn't believed him.

She'd had so little faith in him. In herself.

She folded her arms across her chest, protection against the past. "Are you leaving now?"

"Yes."

"Have a safe trip." She turned toward the door.

"Chloe."

His voice stopped her and she faced him.

"I ran into Grandfather's nurse in the hall. He's awake and asking for you."

"I'll go to him."

Matteo studied her. "Be careful. Stay away from my mother and Ingrid while I'm gone."

"I will. They don't worry me."

Thoughts jumbled, she left the room. Through the lens of time, she knew Ingrid and Valentina had played her. Matteo hadn't supported her against their lies and bullying, magnifying her hurt. Insecure about his love, she'd been easy prey.

"It doesn't matter," she muttered. "We'll soon be divorced." The thought bothered her more than it should have.

* * *

WITH MATTEO away the past two days, Chloe took her meals with Giuseppe in his room. Ingrid had moved into the villa, and Chloe opted for spending time with the elderly man rather than at the table with the two women. She didn't want to admit it, even to herself, but she missed Matteo and couldn't wait until he came back.

She'd settled into a comfortable routine. Most mornings, she read to Giuseppe, and in the afternoons, she helped Francesca. Used to keeping busy, she enjoyed having a schedule, especially one that involved two of her favorite people.

Her phone rang as she left Giuseppe's room after dinner. Smiling over a joke the old man had told, she looked at the phone's screen and connected the call.

"Justin! I meant to call you back, but I got busy. I'm sorry."

"Don't worry about it," he said. "How are you?"

Holding the phone to her ear, Chloe walked down the long hall to her quarters. "I'm good. Giuseppe is the most charming man. I love being with him."

"I hope he's the only one you love being with there."

Surprised at his jealousy, she swallowed. "Yes."

"Any idea when you'll be coming home?" he asked. "It's lonely here without you."

Chloe stepped inside her suite. "I should be back soon, Justin." She listened for a while, then said, "Yes, he'll sign the papers. I'm not worried."

She heard a sharp intake of breath and looked up to find Matteo in the room. His lips were drawn into a thin line. His eyes darkened to thunderclouds, sucking all the life from the area.

"I'll call you later," she said to Justin. "Something's come up. Yes, I promise. Goodbye." She disconnected. "Matteo, when did you get back?"

"So, you miss the boyfriend?"

Chloe resisted the urge to roll her eyes at men and their jealousy. "Of course. Justin's a good friend, and an important part of my life."

"I don't want you talking to him while you're under my roof."

"What?" She threw her phone on the bed. "Who the hell do you think you are to talk to me like that? I'm not your child. I'm here for Giuseppe's sake. You and I have an agreement that doesn't include your ordering me around."

His features relaxed. "I'm sorry. I forget I have no right, not anymore."

"You never had the right to tell me what to do."

"As you liked to remind me."

He smiled, the radiant crooked smile that dissolved her tension and made butterflies swarm in her stomach.

"All those generations of arrogant DiMarco males sometimes comes over me." He chuckled. "None of them dealt with an independent American woman."

"Don't let it happen again." Despite her words, she grinned. She'd always enjoyed their banter.

His soft laugh made the partying butterflies go crazy.

"Have you eaten?" he asked.

"I had dinner a little while ago with Giuseppe."

"Lucia is sending something up for me. Join me for some wine and keep me company while I eat?"

Chloe wanted to say no. "Yes. Okay." The words escaped her mouth before she could stop them.

CHAPTER 10

Matteo and Chloe sat on the suite's patio together. He ate his dinner slowly in an effort to keep her by his side. She'd refused wine and food, and sat quietly drinking a sparkling water. He wanted her attention, wanted her big gray eyes trained on him.

He swallowed some steamed vegetables and sipped his drink. Nothing could wash away the jealousy he'd experienced when he heard her on the phone with her lover. He shouldn't have lashed out at her in that overbearing way. Thinking about Chloe making love with another man had made Matteo's nerves raw. He forced himself to concentrate on the serene gardens and the placid turquoise water, but his regret and hurt found no cessation.

Out of the corner of his eye, he saw Chloe's hand reach over and nab a vegetable off his plate. Lifting a brow, he turned to her.

She laughed and popped the food into her mouth.

"I thought you weren't hungry," he said. "Now, you steal my food."

God knew, he'd missed her playfulness. Unlike any woman he'd known, she'd made life an adventure whenever he was with her. When she tried to grab another vegetable, he placed his hand over hers. "Oh, no, you don't."

Her lips lifted in a smile. "Food tastes better when it's forbidden."

His body tightened. "Lots of things are tastier when they're forbidden." He was rewarded by a pink blush that colored her expressive face.

Chloe looked down at the table, then back to him. "I guess I'll go in now."

"Stay." He hated that he wanted to beg her to be with him, that he chased away their light-hearted teasing.

"I need to go."

Disappointment poured through him as she left. He checked his watch. Late here, but not so late in the States. He wondered if she would call that Justin guy again. He plucked his wine from the table and gripped the stem of the glass before finishing off the drink.

CHLOE CHANGED into yoga pants and a tank top. Taking her phone, she headed downstairs to the patio off the living room and relaxed into a chaise. The ebb and flow of the Mediterranean, like a sonata, kept her company. She should call Justin. It was still early in Philadelphia. Her fingers wouldn't move over the screen. She placed the phone on the small tile-topped table next to her. Folding her arms across her chest, she laid her head back and closed her eyes, letting the fragrance of the summer flowers wrap her in their sweetness.

Matteo. She could no longer deny she still loved him and wanted him. He'd been so ready to let her go two years ago. Through her pregnancy, she'd kept hope alive he'd follow her. In labor, in the hospital, with her parents at her side, she'd finally accepted Matteo no longer loved her.

She'd survived their breakup and her pregnancy when she'd felt so alone. Truth be told, two years later, she'd still held a glimmer of hopefulness Matteo would come for her. He'd finally come to Philadelphia, but only for Giuseppe's sake. Their unsigned divorce papers lay heavy between them. She suspected if not for his grandfather, Matteo would have signed the papers and sent them to her.

Once he signed, she'd tell him about the children and hope he didn't hate her for keeping them from him. Then, she'd go back home. Guilt pulled at her. She needed to ramp up her courage to tell him before he signed the papers. To wait, then run, was cowardly.

Footsteps sounded behind her. Chloe's heart lurched.

"What are you doing out here?" Matteo asked.

She twisted to find him framed by the doorway. "Enjoying the view and the flowers. I love Philadelphia. It's my home, but we have nothing that compares to this."

He lowered himself onto the chaise next to her. "At one time Ravello was your home, but you chose to run with no explanation except a short note. I deserved more than that, Chloe."

His words heightened her regret and uncertainties about her decision. She met his brooding eyes. "I deserved a husband who defended me against his mother and others bent on destroying us. I thought our marriage was irrevocably broken."

"You had no faith in me. You believed lies deliberately told to create doubt, and rumors planted in the gossip magazines to boost sales. You should have stayed and talked to me."

Anger propelled her to stand. "Would you have listened? I tried to get you to discuss our problems, but you wouldn't. You didn't care enough to follow me to Philadelphia." She blinked back tears. She hated for him to see her cry. "I waited for you."

Her back stiff, she went inside.

* * *

SHOCK ROOTED MATTEO to his seat. She'd waited for him? If she knew how many times he almost went to her. Pride, arrogance, stubbornness, and his broken heart had held him from going after the woman he loved. It was too late now. She loved another man.

He didn't know why he'd brought up the old hurts now, but they'd simmered in his mind and heart for two years. He wanted her to know her leaving almost broke him, but his damnable pride wouldn't let him open to her.

Defeat settled over him like a black cloud, obliterating all hope. He pressed his lips together. He was a DiMarco. DiMarcos fought for what they wanted. This time, he would not give up Chloe without a fight.

He stared into the darkness, a plan forming in his mind. He was here. That Justin guy was an ocean away. Location was everything.

The butler brought him the Campari he'd requested, and he sat on the patio as darkness blanketed the sky. Like a bad movie, his mind played over and over the shock and heartbreak of that day two years ago when she'd left him. He'd never before felt such pain, such loss. He hadn't believed he could ever forgive her.

He sipped his drink and stared at the stars twinkling in the heavens and knew he'd forgive Chloe anything if she would stay with him. He threw back his drink, set the empty glass on the table, then pushed up from the chaise and went into the house and to their suite. He found Chloe in bed. Desire hit him, swift and intense. She lay on her side, her eyes closed. Her hair spread out on the pillow, the red strands highlighted in the dim light. He knew she only pretended to sleep.

He took a step forward, ready to climb into bed with her, then stopped. Winning her back demanded finesse and understanding, not cave man antics.

Resigned to do what he must, he went into his dressing room. Another lonely night awaited.

THE NEXT MORNING, Chloe dressed, had breakfast in the kitchen, then went to Giuseppe's quarters. Matteo was gone when she woke. She'd had a restless night, her thoughts and dreams filled with him. She'd heard him come into the room and she'd feigned sleep. A part of her had wanted him to slip into her bed, to make love to her, to hold her and whisper endearments in Italian like he used to.

Exhausted and cranky, she knocked softly on Giuseppe's door. His nurse opened it and waved her in. Giuseppe was sitting at the table in his suite, finishing breakfast.

"Good morning, grandfather." Chloe sat across from him, and at his invitation, poured herself a cup of espresso.

"You look tired today. Are you troubled?" Giuseppe asked.

"I didn't sleep well. That's all."

The old man studied her. "Something is wrong. Did you and Matteo fight?"

She sipped her coffee, needing the caffeine jolt, then set her cup down. "No, nothing like that. Things are happening so fast."

He laid his hand over hers. "Don't worry. Everything will be *va bene*."

"I wish I could believe all will be fine." She hadn't meant to blurt that out. She'd promised herself to always be upbeat around Giuseppe.

"Has my grandson been treating you well?"

At the concern in Giuseppe's eyes, she forced a smile. "Matteo has always been good to me." True. The problems in their marriage were more complicated.

"You look very nice. Do you and Matteo have plans today?"

"I'm helping Francesca again." She brushed a hand over her tan linen pencil skirt, worn with a pale green silk blouse, and beige heels. She'd put her hair up, too, presenting a professional picture.

He set his napkin on the table. "I am tired today. I will miss our reading time, but I need to lie down. I'm sure Francesca could use your help now."

Chloe stood and bent to kiss him on the cheek. "I'll try to come back this evening and read to you. You rest now. I'm anxious to know what further troubles our young Roman senator can get into."

CHAPTER 11

"This place is an unexpected gem." The elderly American woman smiled as Chloe handed her the small bag with her purchases from the gift shop.

"Thank you," Chloe said. "We're glad you found us."

The woman walked away, and Chloe leaned against the counter. They'd been busy all day, keeping her from concentrating on Matteo. Now, at four o'clock, the work and her lack of sleep had her beat. She'd helped Francesca by doing tours, expanding on the brief history of each item. Note cards were placed with the artifacts, but as she'd set up the exhibits, Chloe had in-depth knowledge, which the tourists appreciated. The central piece, the large blue Murano vase, was a crowd pleaser. The vase with 24-karat gold leaf trim was old when Sofia purchased it over fifty years ago. It was now worth thousands of dollars. Good thing the gallery had a state-of-the art security system.

When the young woman who manned the gift shop

had to leave on a family emergency, Chloe stepped in. She'd had a good time waiting on the tourists.

Francesca came up to her. "Looks like it's slowing down. Thanks for your help today."

"I loved it. You've done a tremendous job on publicity. I never thought of targeting the tourist buses that come through Ravello, like the one with the Americans that just left."

"That was Tommaso's idea. He has a marketing degree."

"You make a great pair, complementing each other."

"As do you and Matteo. I would like to visit Philadelphia someday and see your galleria. I hear it is very successful." Francesca beamed. "You are very, how you say, savvy."

"I would love to have you and Tommaso visit. Let's make it happen."

"Francesca, I need you," the student apprentice tour guide called out.

"*Mi scusi.*" Francesca strode toward the young woman.

Chloe leaned her arms on the counter and sighed. Francesca thought she and Matteo complemented each other. Their acting skills exceeded what she would have believed.

She turned her attention to more uplifting thoughts. She was proud of what she'd accomplished in setting up the Sofia DiMarco Gallery here and the Chloe Decker DiMarco Gallery in Philadelphia.

Since she'd been back in Italy, she'd called Janie every day. Janie assured her things were going well, with the help of Chloe's friend, Charli Deveraux. With her art history degree, Charli was a big asset to them.

Charli was saving up money to buy into Chloe's business. Chloe liked having complete control, but she couldn't keep up the pace of twelve-hour days, especially now that the twins were getting older. Her parents deserved their own life. She couldn't expect them to spend their retirement years caring for Joey and Sofie.

Thinking of her intelligent little bundles of non-stop energy, she smiled.

Four-thirty came, and she was free to leave. She traipsed back to the villa, looking forward to resting on one of the patios, a cold glass of wine in hand.

Changed into casual clothes, Chloe settled into a padded chair on the small patio off the study. She liked the intimacy of the smaller space. In these early summer days, darkness fell like a soft shade, and now at five o'clock, the sun still shone brightly over the gardens and Mediterranean. She'd always loved Ravello and the villa, had felt at home here from the first day she arrived, a recent university graduate with a Masters in Art History, anxious about her new, impressive job, and wanting to make her mark as an art expert. When she'd fallen in love with Matteo, she'd believed fate had pushed her to this place of romance and beauty.

Footsteps behind her distracted her, and she looked over her shoulder to see Matteo in the doorway. Wordlessly, they stared at each other. He scanned her, his eyes dark with a challenge that set her pulse racing.

"Federico said you were here. Mind if I join you?" he

asked. "Dinner isn't for a while. I've asked the maid to bring more wine."

"It's your house. You can do what you please." She wanted to bite back the words. Her snarkiness came from her trepidation she would never get him out of her system. Because of the twins, he'd always be in her life. And in her heart.

Instead of taking offense, he laughed and sank onto a chair across from her. His laugh reminded her of Joey. Their son had Matteo's smile. Sofie had his golden-brown eyes. Every time she looked at her children, she was reminded of the love she and Matteo had shared.

Teresa, the maid, entered with a bottle of wine and two glasses on a tray. She set them on the small table between Matteo and Chloe. With a shy smile at Chloe, she curtsied and left.

Chloe raised an eyebrow at Matteo. "Pretty sure of your welcome, weren't you? What if I told you I didn't want you to sit here?"

Grinning, he shrugged. "Like a spoiled child, I would have taken my wine and gone somewhere else, but I knew you wouldn't refuse me."

"Arrogant as always." She couldn't help the smile that hovered over her lips. She finished her drink and set the empty glass on the table.

He poured them each wine from the new bottle, handing a glass to her. "This is a better-quality than the one you were drinking. I thought you'd need it after working at the gallery." He sipped his drink, then set down his glass. "How was it?"

"I loved it. I enjoyed working with Francesca again

and talking to the customers, and especially showing off the exquisite pieces."

He settled into his chair. "I looked around your place in Philadelphia a bit. You're to be commended for what you've done. I understand you've developed your gallery into one of Philadelphia's premier showcases for young talent."

Chloe swallowed a little of the wine, hoping the cool slide of it down her throat would stop the heat she felt on her face. "Thank you. I worked hard, lots of hours, but I had help from my parents, my brothers and their wives, and members of the art community. I've been blessed."

She wanted to tell him she'd worked during her pregnancy and while caring for two infants, but it wasn't time yet to reveal her secret.

If not now, when? a small voice whispered. She ignored it.

"How are things going without you there now?" he asked.

"I've spoken to Janie every day. She's got everything under control. A friend of mine is helping out. She's saving to buy into the gallery. I hate to relinquish complete control but it will be nice to have some free time."

"Running a company by yourself is hard. I found that out after Santino died."

"Giuseppe said you've been working hard."

Matteo held up a hand. "Enough about me. Tell me about your life in Philadelphia."

"You surprise me. I didn't think you cared about my life there."

His eyes held hers. "I'm interested in everything you do. I want to hear how you've lived these past two years." He smiled. "Don't bother to mention Justin or any other boyfriend you've had."

If he only knew Justin was the only man she'd dated, and that she hadn't been intimate with him yet. "I won't discuss Justin or any man because that is none of your business."

He saluted her with his glass. "As you've reminded me many times."

"What do you want to know about me?"

"A day in the life of Chloe Decker DiMarco."

They talked as day gave way to twilight, streaking the sky with purple, pink, and pale yellow, a colorful kaleidoscope designed to restore one's soul.

Matteo listened intently as she described the minutiae of her days, carefully edited to avoid mention of the children. The twins were such a big part of her life, she found it hard to cut them out.

He asked questions that showed his interest, and laughed at her stories of the quirky characters who made up Philadelphia's art scene. Maybe he had changed. He'd always been kind, but he'd had a haughtiness born of generations of aristocratic breeding. He seemed humbler somehow. She remembered what Giuseppe said about Matteo not having time to play.

As darkness draped them, the melody of the sea below lulled her into a peacefulness she hadn't known in a long time.

"Thank you," he said when she'd finished. "We should

get ready for dinner." He stood and held his hand out to help her stand.

She placed her hand in his big one. At his touch, a current of electricity went through her and sparked the feeling she was where she belonged, and with the right man. She stumbled and he caught her to him. Pressed against his taut, muscled chest, longing shimmered through her. Maybe it was the wine she'd drunk, but she threw caution aside and gave in to her craving. She touched the pads of her fingers to his soft, full lips. His scent of sandalwood invited her to feast on his luscious mouth.

She rose up on her toes and kissed him, savoring his essence, and speared her fingers through his dark hair, luxuriating in the silky feel of it. He tasted like wine and desire.

His low groans kindled an answering hunger in her. He cupped the back of her head and deepened the kiss. His tongue sparred with hers. Her belly tightened in response.

Her doubts and anxieties flew away in the flower-scented night. She knew only Matteo and the pleasure she so deeply needed, the love her soul desired.

He released her and framed her face between his palms. The savage gleam in his eyes weakened her knees and she melted against him.

"Chloe." The way he said her name, raw with emotion, took her back to their early days, when they couldn't get enough of each other. She wanted that again.

A shuffling behind them permeated her sexual fog. She

and Matteo turned to the doorway to find an embarrassed Teresa standing there.

"*La cena e servita.*" The maid fled back into the house.

Matteo and Chloe laughed.

"Bad timing," Matteo said. "But since dinner is served, we must go."

"I'm not dressed for dinner." Chloe waved a hand over her khaki pants, white T-shirt, and flat sandals.

"You look beautiful, as always. Don't worry about it." He held out his arm.

She slipped her arm through his.

He leaned in to whisper in her ear. "We'll continue this later."

With his promise ringing in her ears, they headed for the dining room.

Panic and happiness coalesced in Chloe. She and Matteo were rediscovering their love.

CHAPTER 12

Chloe couldn't wait until the tense dinner ended. Giuseppe, begging tiredness, didn't join them this night. Matteo and Chloe sat across from Valentina and Ingrid. The two women conversed together through most of the meal, which was okay with Chloe. Valentina had given Chloe a slight smile when she came to the table. Either Valentina had had a change of heart about Chloe or she was softening her up for whatever cruel plans she had.

Chloe and Matteo said little to each other, but every brush of his hand as she passed him food out of his reach, and the smoldering look in his eyes told her he remembered his promise to finish the kiss they'd started on the patio.

Federico came into the room and whispered in Matteo's ear. Matteo threw his napkin on the table and stood. He stared down at Chloe. "I have an important call that can't wait. I'll be as quick as I can."

He didn't look at the others before leaving.

Valentina huffed as Matteo left. "He should not leave during dinner. Family dinners are most important."

Chloe ignored her, but Ingrid touched Valentina's arm. "Do not worry, Valentina. He forgets his manners. He has been influenced by Americans who behave like barbarians and don't know how to dress for dinner."

Picking up her glass of wine, Chloe sipped, set the glass down slowly, and stared Ingrid in the eyes. "We Americans have good manners, but sometimes we're with those for whom manners mean nothing."

The women widened their eyes, shock tightening their features. To Chloe's surprise, Valentina's lips tilted in a smile she quickly suppressed.

Chloe stood. "Good evening to you both." She walked slowly out, resisting the impulse to run as fast as she could.

When she reached the hall, she took a long, deep breath. Those women plucked her last nerve. Thankfully, she'd soon be rid of them.

Rid of Matteo, too?

The thought froze her with one foot on the bottom step on her way upstairs. She recognized there was too much pain and distrust between them, but because of Joey and Sofie, Matteo would always be in her life. And she was glad of it.

She'd check on Giuseppe before going to her suite. Thank God Valentina and Ingrid had rooms in a separate wing of the sprawling house.

She knocked softly on Giuseppe's door and slipped inside when he called out to come in.

He sat on an upholstered chaise in his sitting room, reading. Smiling, Chloe went to him.

"Giuseppe, I'm surprised you're up and reading. I thought you were tired."

"Not too tired to read. Sit, child." Removing his glasses and closing his book, he waved her to a chair across from him.

"What is your book?" she asked.

He shrugged. "A best-selling thriller by an Italian author. Not as good as expected." He grinned. "And not as good as the misadventures of our favorite Roman senator."

Crossing her legs at the ankles, Chloe relaxed into the chair. "I promised to help Francesca again tomorrow, but it's not until afternoon. I'll visit you after breakfast and we can read together."

"I look forward to it."

He stared at her, his eyes intense. "What bothers you, child?"

"Nothing for you to worry about." For Giuseppe's sake, she would pretend all was okay. She couldn't tell him about her conflicted feelings toward Matteo. Or her worries about what Matteo would do when she told him about the children.

"I am happy you and my grandson are together. I had hoped you and he would have children before I leave this world." Sadness flitted over Giuseppe's face. "I suppose it is too late now."

Guilt punched her in the stomach. She could ease the old man's worries and tell him about the twins.

She had to tell Matteo first.

As if a noose tightened around her neck, she swallowed.

"I have kept up with you since you left," Giuseppe said.

"You have?"

"My friends tell me your galleria is very successful, the talk among the artist class in Philadelphia." He smiled, looking pleased with himself. "Matteo taught me to use a computer, and I sometimes look on that Google thing to see which exhibits you are showing."

A chill shivered up her spine. She kept references to the children and pictures of them off the internet and social media. She hoped Giuseppe hadn't heard or read something that led him to discover her secret.

She tamped down her apprehension and gave him a shaky smile. "The gallery has been a labor of love, and I've had good support."

"Tell me about the Chloe Decker DiMarco Gallery. The Google only gives me pictures."

They talked another twenty minutes, with Chloe telling him tales of the early days when she bought the business from the former owner, who was retiring. With the money she'd saved from her salary as director of the Sofia DiMarco Gallery, financial help from her parents, bank loans, and hard work, she made it her own. As with Matteo, she edited out mentions of Joey and Sofie. Giuseppe listened intently.

"I would have given you any amount of money you needed," he said when she finished. With a clucking noise, he shook his head. "You can be as prideful and stubborn as my grandson."

"I couldn't take money from you or Matteo." She touched his hand across the table. "The artists and patrons you referred to me were tremendously helpful. They were more valuable than money."

"I wanted to help."

"I'll always be grateful to you."

His gaze met hers. "Chloe, my dear, you're family. We DiMarcos care for our own."

A flush spread from her neck to her face. She'd never known her grandfathers. Keeping Joey and Sofie from Matteo meant keeping them from this kind man who'd always treated her like a granddaughter.

He yawned, giving her a reason to escape from the guilt threatening to overtake her.

She stood. "You're tired. Do you want me to call your nurse?" His nurse had a room in the servants' quarters on the third floor. Of the regular staff, only Federico lived in the villa, with rooms on the same floor. The other servants resided in Ravello.

Giuseppe waved a hand. "I'm not ready for bed yet. I want to read a little more."

Chloe kissed his cheek. "I'll see you tomorrow morning."

She left his quarters and headed to the rooms she shared with Matteo. Halfway down the hall, the clicking of high heels on the marble floor made her stop and turn around. Ingrid strode quickly toward her, determination on her face. Dismay washed over Chloe. She wanted to flee, but she wouldn't show weakness to the Swede.

Tapping a foot, Chloe folded her arms across her chest, putting on the pose of impatience. "In the wrong wing, aren't you?" she asked when the blonde reached her.

"I am looking for you," Ingrid said.

"You found me."

Ingrid smirked. "*Imburrare il vecchio.*"

Loosely translated, Ingrid accused Chloe of buttering up the old man. "What are you saying? I love Giuseppe. He's a grandfather to me."

"I know what you're up to," the Swede said. "Your plan won't work. You and Matteo don't fool me with your *reconciliation.*"

Chloe's heart leapt to her throat. If Ingrid discovered they pretended to reunite, the knowledge would hurt Giuseppe.

"What?" Chloe said.

Ingrid stepped closer. Chloe held her ground.

"Now that Giuseppe is dying, Matteo is conspiring to take all his money, leaving nothing for Valentina." The blonde spit the words out. "Matteo never cared for you. How much money did he promise from Giuseppe's estate for you to come back?"

"You're crazy. I'm not standing here listening to you." Chloe started to walk away.

Ingrid grabbed her arm, stopping her.

Chloe whirled around and flared her nostrils. "Take. Your. Hand. Off. Me."

The other woman removed her hand. "Matteo is mine. He was always mine." With disgust on her face, she swept a hand down to indicate Chloe's body. "You are an American boor. Go away from here. Or else."

Red-hot rage burned through Chloe. "Are you threatening me? And for the record, Matteo was never yours." She turned on her heel and strode away, anger driving her down the hall to her rooms.

In her suite, she suppressed the urge to slam the door. She wasn't a teen, but a grown woman who could handle mean girl Ingrid.

Chloe leaned against the closed door, breathing heavily. "Matteo!" she called out. Silence greeted her. Thank God. She didn't want to deal with him right now.

Taking off her jewelry as she walked, she deposited them on the dresser. She studied herself in the mirror. Rage had reddened her face. She hated that her feelings showed so easily.

"You need to ignore Ingrid. She's bluffing." Chloe rubbed a hand down her face. She wouldn't let Ingrid hurt her this time around.

Valentina and Ingrid no longer had power over her. She had a life, a thriving business, and, most of all, children whom she adored and vowed to protect.

CHAPTER 13

Chloe, wearing cotton pajamas, sat at her dressing table brushing her hair when the door opened to Matteo. Her pulse skyrocketed and her hand holding the brush stilled.

He walked to stand behind her. Their eyes met in the mirror.

"Let me do that." He took the brush and began running it through her hair.

She leaned her head back, letting the eroticism of Matteo's touch send scorching heat along her nerve endings. Languid and content, she sighed.

"Why do you have on little-girl pajamas?" he asked, his voice raspy. "You used to wear sheer silk that I could easily take off you."

"Those days are gone, Matteo."

"They don't have to be."

His words threw cold water on her libido. She kept a secret from him that would squelch any hope of a real reunion between them.

And there was Ingrid's threat. She wouldn't tell him, but she worried how much Ingrid knew and what trouble the blonde could make.

Chloe took the brush from him, set it on the vanity, and stood. "I need to sleep."

He skimmed his palms down her arms and took both her hands in his. Looking deeply into her eyes, he said, "Sleep with me."

"We can't. There's too much unresolved between us. We must talk, but I'm not ready. Give me time."

The surprise that flashed over his eyes quickly changed to hurt. "Is it the boyfriend in Philadelphia? Are you in love with him?"

The naked vulnerability in his question provoked a flicker of hope in her. His pride and stubbornness had softened. He'd matured, and so had she.

She freed herself and stepped back. "Justin is a good friend, and that's all."

"You're my wife until our divorce is final." He spoke softly with no hint of pride.

"You promised to sign the papers if I came here with you."

His features tensed. "Don't worry. I'll keep my word. Good night."

He pivoted and walked out.

She sank back onto the vanity seat. She'd done the right thing, sending him away.

Any future they had together depended on his forgiving her deception.

* * *

Matteo sat in his office, an untouched glass of Irish whiskey in front of him. Frustrated with his need for Chloe, he grabbed his drink and finished it in one swallow, plunking the empty glass onto the desk. Regret and the whiskey burned his throat. He shouldn't have let her go, should have been a better husband.

Despite his decision to win her back, he'd come on too strong and scared her. He needed to treat her more gently, to make her realize she belonged with him.

His mind wandered to the day he returned from a business trip to Paris, two years ago, the day his life and marriage unraveled. Tired and missing his wife, he ran up to their suite as soon as he entered the villa. Chloe waited for him, her face tight and her arms folded across her chest, spoiling for a fight. She'd accused him of cheating on her with Ingrid and others. He'd denied all the charges, but his damn pride and conceit kept him from denying with any force. He'd told himself if Chloe loved him, she'd believe him and not ugly lies.

She'd said they needed to talk things out. He'd disagreed and spent the night in one of the spare rooms in the villa. The next day, he'd been in Rome on business. When he returned, Chloe had gone, leaving only a brief note and her engagement ring. He'd been lonely before he met her and lonely again when she left.

His heart had never healed.

He pounded a fist on the table, sending his empty glass wobbling. He was a successful businessman, heir to one of Italy's great fortunes, and he was mooning over a woman like an inexperienced teen.

Chloe wasn't any woman. She was the woman he loved. The woman he'd lost due to his misplaced egotism.

* * *

MID-MORNING, three days after her confrontation with Ingrid, Chloe hurried down the hall to Giuseppe's quarters, already missing Matteo who left early that morning for another business trip. Since refusing his lovemaking, he'd been cordial but made no move to kiss or even touch her again. She told herself she was glad, but deep down, she wanted his attention and caresses.

Her business at home, under the guidance of Janie and Charli, was running smoothly. While that made her happy and secure, it brought the realization she wasn't needed there every minute. The twins appeared to be doing fine without her, too. At home, she moved through her days quickly, constantly working, thinking the gallery and her children couldn't get along without her. Her ego took a hit that she'd been wrong.

The door to Giuseppe's suite was open and she walked in. Dressed in a blue button-down shirt and dark pants, Giuseppe sat in his wheelchair, a deep-blue blanket spread across his legs. She'd promised to take him to the Sofia DiMarco Gallery today.

"Good morning." She kissed his cheek. "Ready to go?"

He smiled. "I always love visiting my Sofia's collection."

She scanned the room. "Where's your nurse?"

He waved a hand. "I don't need her. I am energized

today." His eyes twinkled and he projected exuberance, like the spirited man she used to know.

Francesca ran to open the doors when she saw them. "Ciao, Signore DiMarco. Ciao, Chloe."

"Good morning, Francesca," Giuseppe said. "You look pretty."

"Grazie." Francesca's face pinked at his compliment.

The obvious affection between Francesca and the elderly man sparked a flash of jealousy in Chloe. If she'd not run off to Philadelphia, the Sofia DiMarco Gallery would still be hers to run as she pleased. And the villa would be her home. She and Giuseppe would be closer.

And she and Matteo would be loving parents raising the twins together.

On the other hand, if she'd stayed in Italy, she wouldn't have her successful business in Philadelphia, something that gave her tremendous confidence.

A tourist bus stopped and discharged the passengers, dragging her mind from her conflicted thoughts.

Francesca and her staff lined up to greet the new customers. When a group went immediately to the blue Murano vase, Giuseppe motioned for Chloe to wheel him over to them.

For the next forty-five minutes, he entertained the tourists with clever and amusing anecdotes about the pieces. Laughter and claps signified how much the visitors enjoyed him.

Customers surged the gift shop. Chloe offered to help the clerk while Francesca wheeled Giuseppe around, the tourists following him like the Pied Piper.

Chloe managed to study Giuseppe as she worked. He

hadn't been this animated since the first time she'd come to Ravello. His hearty laugh mingled with the customers' as he joked with them. She half expected him to leave the wheelchair and walk around with the springy step of a much younger man.

Something didn't add up. Giuseppe didn't appear to be the fragile old man he had when she came back a few weeks ago. Maybe her being here had helped invigorate him. She'd asked Matteo to explain what was wrong with his grandfather. He'd met with Giuseppe's doctor, but due to privacy issues, the doctor couldn't reveal anything of Giuseppe's condition. And Giuseppe refused to sign the papers giving Matteo access to his medical records.

A kernel of doubt opened in her mind. She and Matteo were living a lie. Maybe they weren't the only ones.

CHAPTER 14

Giuseppe joined them at dinner that night, again the feeble, stooped-over old man, not the effervescent one at the gallery earlier. Strained conversations accompanied the dinner, with Valentina and Ingrid more quiet than usual. Valentina gave Chloe a small smile when they sat down. Either the woman had truly changed her opinion of Chloe or she was trying to gaslight her.

Back from his business trip, Matteo looked exhausted, with fine lines around his eyes and mouth. Chloe flexed her fingers, resisting the urge to skim them over his haggard face and help him relax, as she'd done early in their marriage. She'd lost that right when she left him.

After dinner, Giuseppe's nurse took him back to his room. Chloe turned to Matteo. "Let's stroll in the gardens. The night is beautiful, and a walk will do us both good."

Surprise flashed across his face before he smiled the crooked smile that always made her heart jump. Their son, with the same smile, was already a charmer like his dad.

Thinking of her children brought the usual anxiety. She would tell him about the children, but not tonight. Matteo was too tired to deal with that news.

Valentina nodded at them as they left the table. "Chloe is right, Matteo. You look tired. A walk will do you good."

Surprise at Valentina's statement accompanied Chloe as they went outside. She wanted to have a good relationship with Matteo's mother. Maybe that was possible at last. Despite their differences, the woman was her children's grandmother.

When they arrived at the gardens, Matteo took Chloe's hand. She didn't pull away. Walking hand-in-hand with the man she'd always loved, the night birds singing their lullabies, and the full moon leaving a trail on the calm surface of the Mediterranean, peace covered her like gossamer silk.

Although homesick for the twins, her parents, her gallery, she knew she was where she needed to be at this moment.

They sat on a stone bench overlooking the sea. Matteo released her and scrubbed a hand over his face.

"Tough trip?" she asked.

"More than most. I'll survive." He turned to her and placed his fingers under her chin to tilt her face until their eyes met. "I'm glad you suggested this walk. The gardens always refresh me."

"Me, too."

He moved slightly away and focused on the water.

"I took Giuseppe to the gallery today," she said.

Matteo slid his gaze to her. "He loves that place."

"He seemed a different person, vibrant, laughing, not old and sickly at all."

"The excursion did him good."

Chloe moved back in her seat. The hard marble pressed into her back, a reminder not to become complacent. Matteo and she had issues to resolve. She inhaled the sweet, calming perfume of the flowers and trees. "Does Giuseppe trust his doctor. Did he get a second opinion?"

"Dr. Palmarella has treated my grandfather for many years. Grandfather saw no need for a second opinion."

"Something's not right."

"Being with you at the gallery energized him. He's an old man. Don't hope for a cure that will never happen."

She sighed. "I'm worrying over nothing."

"Let's talk of other things. I've been working hard lately and I need to get away for a rest. I think you could use one too."

"What are you saying?"

"Spend a few days on the *Sofia* with me."

She looked down, hiding her surprise at his words. The yacht. They'd spent many passion-filled hours making love in the large cabin while the vessel cut smoothly through the waters of the Bay of Naples. She'd loved him with joyful abandon, willing to do whatever he wanted, desperate to learn how to excite him as he excited her.

"Chloe?"

She raised her eyes to him. "The *Sofia*?"

He rubbed the knuckles of one hand gently over her face. "You surely remember the times we had there, when we were so in love?"

"I came here for Giuseppe. You and I are not reconciled. I can't go on the yacht alone with you."

"We won't be alone. The crew will be onboard."

She laughed. "The discreet crew I almost never saw, although I'm sure they heard us."

"The ship has three cabins." His expression grew serious. "You can take the main stateroom and I'll use one of the smaller ones. We will go as friends, out for a relaxing time."

She could use the break. He couldn't seduce her back to his bed. Unless she wanted him to.

"Okay. I'll go."

CHAPTER 15

Early the next morning, Matteo helped Chloe into the passenger side of his dark blue Maserati. She clicked on her seat belt as he climbed into the driver's side and buckled up.

"I like this blue color. When did you trade in your black one?"

He started the engine and didn't look at her. "Soon after you left. The old one held too many memories."

She stared at his strong profile. He'd traded in the car he loved because of her? His gesture touched her heart and opened a sliver of hope in her.

They spoke about the weather, the scenery, and art as Matteo guided them to the Amalfi Coast and Positano, the popular, crowded beach town where the *Sofia* docked. Chloe was glad they didn't talk about their future or their past. She wanted to kick back and relish this time away from the villa.

The narrow roads and turns along the coast didn't

scare her today. The heavy traffic kept everyone driving at a safe speed, at least safe for Italy.

"I'd almost forgotten how beautiful it is along here." Like a woman starved, Chloe's gaze devoured the houses in every color of the rainbow that hugged the steep cliffs. Wild flowers marched like colorful gems to the turquoise sea below.

In a little over an hour, they reached Positano. Matteo turned down a winding road clogged with vehicles of all shapes and sizes. Flags, furling and unfurling in the breeze, hung from the brightly painted houses. Sailboats and fishing boats bobbed in the emerald waters. Cars jostled for space, the drivers on the lookout for parking spots.

Matteo pulled onto a small road leading toward the marina. The guard at the booth opened the gate for them and waved them in. The large white yacht rode gently on the water, its flag with the DiMarco coat of arms fluttering. Chloe drew a contented breath and scanned the proud vessel. As the twins got older, she imagined they'd spend time here with Matteo. Sofie would squeal with delight at the name *Sofia* painted on the side. Although named for Matteo's grandmother, their daughter would think Matteo named the yacht for her.

Chloe smiled thinking of the children. Reality bit into her fantasy. The twins might come here with Matteo, but she would not. She and Matteo would be divorced.

He helped her out of the car as a crew member came down the gangplank and opened the trunk to pull out their luggage. They planned to stay one night so each packed lightly. Choosing to enjoy her time on the beautiful ship, Chloe threw aside her anxiety at spending the night alone here with Matteo. The crew would be aboard, but they were quiet and discreet, as she'd learned the many times she and Matteo had made wild love onboard.

Lorenzo, the captain, greeted them as they walked onto the deck. He tipped his hat and smiled at Chloe. "*Benvenuta, Signora DiMarco. 'E bello rivederti.*"

"Grazie, Lorenzo. It's good to see you, too," Chloe answered in English.

The men talked together, their Italian too rapid for her to follow along.

With a salute for Matteo, the captain walked away.

Matteo turned to Chloe. "Our bags are in the cabins and lunch is ready on the upper deck."

Shouts in Italian as the crew readied the large vessel for sailing accompanied Chloe and Matteo like a concert as they enjoyed lunch of fresh swordfish, salad, and an exquisite pinot grigio.

Chloe popped a piece of fish in her mouth and closed her eyes, savoring the deliciousness of the swordfish, caught in the nearby waters. The *Sofia's* chef, owner of one of Positano's best restaurants, made himself available to the DiMarco family whenever they needed his services.

"You like the food?" Matteo said, humor in his voice.

She opened her eyes and blinked. Matteo watched her in amusement.

"The food is to die for." She reached for her glass and sipped. "The wine is to die for, too." She set down her glass and spread her arms. "This yacht is to die for, and so is the scenery."

"What about the company? Am I to die for also?"

Their eyes met, and something hot and pulsing sparked between them.

"Yes, you too." The words slipped from her.

"Thank you."

Trying to get some control over her emotions, she speared another piece of fish.

Matteo laughed. "I always loved how much you enjoy food. So different from the emaciated models we use in our company's magazines."

The thought of the models, actresses, and royals Matteo courted the past two years, as the gossip rags reported, darkened Chloe's good mood like clouds covering the sun. With effort, she forced herself to concentrate on the flamboyant houses riding the cliffs, and the bathers enjoying the beaches below. She needed to get a grip, to not let the past interfere with her enjoyment of this day.

"Chloe."

Matteo's softly spoken word drew her attention to him. He reached across the table to place a hand over hers. "I never cheated on you," he said, as if reading her mind. "From the first time I saw you in the plaza at Ravello, I never wanted another woman."

She finished her wine and set the glass on the tiled table. "I know you had to look like you were with all those women for publicity before we met. I saw the pictures of you and the European princess in Prague cuddling each other. We were married then." She fought the onslaught of old hurts.

When she tried to pull away, he held onto her hand, his face tight.

"I made a mistake, a big one. She did a photo shoot for the swimsuit issue for our sports magazine. We went to dinner to celebrate a successful campaign, and both of us drank too much. She came on to me, and I didn't discourage her." Sadness flitted across his face. "But, Chloe, nothing more than flirtation happened. She wanted to take it further but I came to my senses. I loved you. I couldn't bed another woman."

"Why didn't you explain all this to me at the time? You became angry when I questioned you. That made me believe the pictures of you two together didn't lie."

He released her hand and blew out a breath. "As my wife, I expected you to have unconditional faith in me."

"A little reassurance from you would have helped."

"I was too proud for my own good." He refilled their glasses. "Let us enjoy this superb food and the gentle breeze and speak of other things. The past is done."

They finished their lunch in silence, although Chloe's thoughts tumbled through her head like the wild flowers clinging to the bluffs and shoreline. Matteo was right. She'd believed the lies planted by Valentina and Ingrid and the photos in the gossip mags. Her own insecurities about Matteo made it easy for her to doubt him and his love. When she saw the pictures of him and the princess laughing and sitting close, cracks formed in her heart. Finding Ingrid in his bed in Paris completed the shattering of her heart.

Matteo had refused to discuss their problems. He'd closed down every time she wanted to talk.

Chloe drank more wine, as if she could drown her hurts. As Matteo had stated, the past was done.

After lunch, the boat docked near a pristine section of beach. They changed into their swimsuits and rode in the dinghy to the shore. One of the crew piloted the small boat, and after letting them off, he promised to be back in two hours.

During their marriage, they'd loved coming to this beach, spending hours swimming and sunbathing. She wondered why Matteo decided to come here today. She suspected he was seducing her with reminiscences of their happy times together. The thought excited and scared her.

They spread a blanket on the sand, and Matteo helped Chloe off with her wrap. His hands skimmed her shoulders and down her arms, sending waves of pleasure through her. His hungry gaze swept her bikini-clad body. "You are more beautiful than I remember."

Maybe she should have worn her one-piece suit.

"Let's go for a swim," she said.

He pulled off his T-shirt, exposing his broad chest and six-pack abs. A scattering of dark hair covered his smooth muscled skin.

"You still work out." The words spilled out of her. Her face heated.

He grinned and took her hand. "Let's go."

They ran together into the water. They swam as far as they dared, then headed back to shore.

Laughing, they dried themselves and sat on the blanket.

"I haven't swum since I left," she said, and immediately regretted her words. She hadn't wanted to bring up the past.

He slipped on his sunglasses and leaned back on his

elbows, his face turned to the sun. "You have been too busy?"

"With my business, and other things." That damn prickly guilt hit her with the force of a rough surf. Now would be a good time to tell Matteo about the twins. Unease froze her vocal cords. She didn't want to ruin the perfection of this moment.

"I've been preoccupied with work, too," he said. "Even before he died, Uncle Santino had almost run the company into bankruptcy with his elaborate spending."

"How did he die? He wasn't very old."

Matteo sat up and chuckled. "Heart attack while in bed with his latest mistress, a twenty-year-old. I suppose she had too much energy for him."

"I'm not glad he died, but that sounds like the way he'd go."

Matteo shrugged. "That he died in a young woman's bed surprised no one."

"Ingrid is on the hunt for a new benefactor."

"She's not important. Let's not mar the day by talking about her."

He pulled the picnic basket toward them and opened it to a bottle of rose′ wine and two glasses. "Swimming made me thirsty."

He passed a glass of wine to her.

Their hands touched. A spark traveled up her arm. She raised her gaze to his. The sunglasses hid his eyes, but she felt desire pulsing from him. She would need all her willpower to resist his pull.

CHAPTER 16

Chloe relaxed on the blanket and lifted her face to the sun, her long hair streaming behind her. Matteo yearned to take her in his arms and make love to her here on the beach.

He sipped wine and fought his libido. He'd promised her they'd spend the day and night as friends. If he would win her trust again, he had to keep his baser instincts in check.

Although he thought of her constantly the past two years, he'd resisted the urge to check her out online. He didn't want to see pictures of her with other men.

She sat straighter. "Giuseppe told me you've been working especially hard lately. I hadn't realized what Santino did to the company. But you're good now, right?"

Matteo set his empty glass back into the basket. "We're good." Chloe had always taken an interest in his work. That she still cared gave him hope.

She studied him. "You've changed, Matteo."

He chuckled. "If you mean my gray hairs, yes."

"That's not what I meant, and the little bit of gray makes you look distinguished."

"Thank you."

"You're much more serious now."

"Being solely responsible for the company my grandparents started grounded me in every way. I want Giuseppe to be proud of me."

Chloe placed her hand over his on the blanket. "He's very proud of you. You must know that."

Her kindness wrapped around his heart. She'd always been a calming influence over him. He'd not appreciated her until she was gone. He hoped it wasn't too late to win her back.

The sun lowered in the sky, bringing a cooling breeze. The sparkle in Chloe's eyes called to him. He slipped off his sunglasses and reached for her to draw her close. He lay back, pulling her on top of him. At the feel of her breasts, barely covered by the small pieces of fabric, his libido roared to life.

"Chloe." Her name tore from his throat.

He captured her lips. She tasted like sun and wine. Their tongues tangled. He ran his hands over her nearly-naked back. She was a goddess, come from the sea. He untied her top and pulled it off her, throwing it onto the blanket. Her bare breasts pressed against his chest. The sun, the sand, the surf, his beautiful wife. His flesh burned where her sun-kissed skin touched him.

"Matteo." Her softly spoken word, filled with longing, floated on the salt-scented breeze.

He lifted her and lay her on the blanket, positioning himself over her.

Shouting permeated his sensual fog. He peered over her shoulder to find the dinghy coming for them.

"Chloe, we won't be alone soon."

She squinted toward the water, then rolled away. Her face colored a pretty shade of pink. With trembling fingers, she tried to put her bikini top on. He took it from her and tied it in place, then kissed her cleavage, eliciting a low groan from her.

Reluctantly releasing her, he stood and waved to the small boat, then helped her up.

She grabbed her wrap and slipped it on.

"You okay?" he asked.

"Just embarrassed." She glanced at his groin. "It's pretty obvious we almost made love here on the beach."

He kissed her lightly on the lips. "Don't be ashamed. We *are* married."

* * *

Back on the yacht, Chloe showered and changed into white linen pants and a pale blue shirt. She applied a minimum of makeup. She didn't need much because the sun gave her skin a glow. She loved the way her body felt after a day in the sunshine—languid, melty, and sensual.

Brushing her hair, she studied herself in the mirror. She suspected Matteo had a lot to do with her skin's glow and the excitement she couldn't tamp down.

Matteo.

She set her brush onto the vanity table and dropped into the nearest chair. If the dinghy hadn't come back when it did, she knew with certainty she and Matteo would have made love. In public. She'd been saved from making a huge mistake. Why did she feel so…cheated?

The bedside clock told her it was time to meet him on the upper deck for cocktails. She hurried out of the cabin.

Matteo, wearing a loose white shirt, jeans, and sandals, lounged on the padded bench on deck, a bottle of wine and a cheese platter on the table in front of him.

He stood when he saw her. His appreciative gaze heated her more than the sunshine.

"You look refreshed." He patted the spot next to him, and she sat. He sat close, too close for her weak willpower.

"We both needed this respite," he said.

"It's been a wonderful day. You're right. I needed this." She accepted a glass of white wine from him.

She sipped her drink and plucked a fat, juicy grape from the platter. She popped the grape in her mouth and closed her eyes, savoring its sweetness. She opened her eyes to Matteo watching her. "This is so delicious. I've forgotten how fresh and sweet fruit is here at this time of year."

"You are delicious," he said.

At his words and the raw longing in his voice, Chloe's hand froze with her drink midway to her mouth. She set the glass onto the table. "What happened on the beach can't happen again. We are not reconciled. Once you sign those divorce papers, we'll no longer be married. We can't let the desire we evidently still feel for each other paint the truth. Our marriage didn't work."

She'd had to say the words, but inside she was screaming. She'd wanted him to make love to her, craved his possession, his touch, his whispered endearments.

His attention on her never wavered. Hurt flashed over his features, to disappear in an instant, replaced by indifference that tore her soul. She didn't want him indifferent to her. Yet, it would be better if he were.

"If that's what you want," he said. "You can't deny the passion between us still burns brightly."

"We fool ourselves if we think we can give in to our… our needs and come out unscathed. What's done is done. We've moved on."

Without a word, he poured another drink and stared beyond her to the shore.

She fought her emotions that told her to go to him, to kiss his beautiful face, to tell him how much she wanted him. How much she loved him.

CHAPTER 17

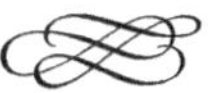

They arrived at the palazzo late the next day. Neither spoke much on the ride back, as if they'd said all they had to on the *Sofia*.

Lying in bed that night, trying to sleep, Chloe replayed the past two days. She heard Matteo in the sitting room moving around. She imagined he felt restless also.

She loved being with him on the yacht, maybe loved it too much. Much as she'd wanted to make love with him, she was glad they didn't, glad she'd made herself clear—they had no chance at reconciliation and needed to move on, especially when she told him about the children. Sadness, regret, and guilt wrapped around her heart.

Soon, she'd go home. Away from Ravello, from Matteo.

Sleep eluded her. She practiced deep breathing and meditation, and finally her eyelids grew heavy. Too soon, sunlight nudged her awake. Silence greeted her. She assumed Matteo rose earlier and left. Chloe inhaled the honied scent of flowers drifting through the opened patio doors. She stretched and sat up. She'd promised to help out at the gallery again today.

It was too early to call home. During her break, she'd phone the twins.

The gallery bustled with customers when Chloe arrived. She waved to Francesca and the staff, all working diligently.

Francesca excused herself from a group of tourists and approached Chloe. "You are just in time for a tour bus that is expected any minute. I worried I had no one to show them around."

"I'm glad to help any way I can."

That busload of tourists and another kept Chloe too busy to think about Matteo and their problems. Lunch break came, and she took her phone outside to make her call.

Chloe punched in the number and waited for her mom to answer.

"Hey, Mom. Everything okay? Are the twins up? I really need to talk to them."

Her mom laughed. "We're all good. Don't worry. They've been asking for you. They're up. I'll put you on speaker and you can talk to both at the same time."

When her mom told the children she was on the phone, their delighted squealing made Chloe's eyes moisten.

"Mommy!" they said in unison.

"Home?" Joey asked.

"Soon, baby. I love you and Sofie."

"Love mommy," Sofie said.

They talked for ten minutes, the kids telling her in

their limited vocabulary about their fun at the park the day before.

The twins grew quiet, as if talking exhausted them. In the background, she heard her mom tell them to say goodbye.

"Bye, mommy," they said.

"Goodbye, sweeties. You be good for Grandmom."

Her mom got back on the line. "All that talking and excitement tired them out. They need their baths now and a nap."

Heart heavy, Chloe said her goodbyes to her mom and disconnected the call. She wanted to go home to her babies.

As things settled down late in the day, Valentina came through the doors. Chloe plastered a smile on her face and approached her mother-in-law.

"Welcome, Valentina. What brings you here?"

"I plan to give some friends a private showing soon. I want to look around before then."

"I'll be glad to show you."

"If you wish."

Chloe vowed to be cordial to the woman. After all, she'd warmed to her lately. Valentina was the twins' grandmother, and they couldn't keep her away from her grandchildren. With Matteo's help, they could keep Valentina's worst instincts from hurting the children.

Provided Matteo wasn't furious with Chloe for keeping them from him. That was a constant worry.

The older woman strode toward the blue Murano vase, encased in a plastic, break-proof case. "A shame we can't touch this and experience all its beauty."

Chloe stood next to her. "If we allowed customers to handle this, it could break. No one wants that."

"The piece's value has increased greatly since Sofia bought it."

"I'm aware of its value."

"It would be too bad if anything happened to it."

Chills skittered up Chloe's spine at what sounded like a thinly veiled threat. She imagined a Mafia boss saying the same thing. "I assure you this piece and the others are well-protected by the state-of-the art security system I had set up."

"Of course." Valentina pivoted on her high heels. "Let's see what else is here." She walked away.

Shaking her head, Chloe followed. There would be no reason for the woman to threaten the valuable vase. Chloe reminded herself to ask Francesca if she regularly changed the security code.

Valentina went to each exhibit, asking questions about the artifacts. Finally, the tour over, she turned to Chloe and smiled.

"Thank you. You know a lot about the items. I appreciate your showing me around."

Chloe smiled, fighting to hide her surprise at the woman's friendliness. "You're welcome."

Valentina glanced away, then back to Chloe. "You know I wasn't pleased when my son married you. I realize I treated you badly before, which wasn't fair to you. My son has been unhappy these past two years. Since you've come back, he smiles more and the stress is gone from his face. Despite everything, I love my son. Much as it pains me to admit it, you're good for him."

"Thank you. I appreciate your saying that."

The other woman turned and walked out, leaving Chloe to stare after her. That was as close to an apology she would get from Valentina. A kernel of warmth toward Matteo's mother bloomed in Chloe.

Hope lightened her steps as she made her way to the back of the gallery. Maybe there was a chance for her and Matteo after all. She would tell him about the twins and pray he could forgive her.

With Matteo still away at dinner time, Chloe, tired from her day, and missing him, took her meal in her suite.

After dinner, she walked to Giuseppe's room, at his invitation, to share wine with him. She and Giuseppe settled onto the patio, and she poured red wine and handed him a glass.

He held it up in salute. "To the granddaughter of my heart."

Her ever-present guilt rose up like a Phoenix from the ashes. She wanted to tell him about the twins, and she would as soon as she told Matteo. Coward that she was, she kept putting off the truth.

"Thank you, grandfather." They clinked glasses.

The outer door opened. They looked over.

Matteo, loosening his tie, walked toward them and smiled. "I suspected I'd find you two together. Mind if I join you?"

"Of course not, my son. Sit. Have some wine. Chloe and I are enjoying the view and each other's company."

Matteo slipped off his jacket and placed it over a nearby chair, then sat next to Chloe.

"You look tired," she said. "Hard day at work?"

He shrugged. "Nothing I can't handle. How was your day?"

"I worked with Francesca. I always enjoy helping out."

He poured himself a glass of wine.

"You work too hard," Giuseppe said to Matteo.

"Someone has to do it, Grandfather, and I don't mind."

The time passed quickly. The three of them finished off two bottles of dark, rich Chianti.

Chloe settled back in her chair, pleasantly buzzed from the alcohol. Darkness descended, bringing the usual cacophony of night insects.

Giuseppe grinned. "Seeing you together is better for my old heart than any medical treatments my doctor can give me. Love shines between you."

Chloe kept her face blank and slid a glance at Matteo. Their eyes met, and she knew his thoughts mirrored hers. They were deceiving this kindly old man.

She sat up before she blurted out the truth behind their reconciliation. She needed to get home, and she had to prepare them. "I have to go back to Philadelphia very soon. I don't want to leave you, Giuseppe, but I have a business that needs me." *And children.*

Shock registered on Matteo's face, but he said nothing.

"I don't want you to leave, child, but I understand about business," Giuseppe said. "You will be back, no, once you take care of things?"

The hopeful expression on the old man's face twisted like a knife in her stomach. "I'll be back, Grandfather." Another lie to add to her sins.

"You must take the company jet," Giuseppe said. "You can get to Philadelphia and back more quickly that way."

"I don't want to put anyone out. Matteo might need the jet for business. I'll book a commercial flight."

"A commercial flight?" Matteo said, an edge to his words. "Our plane is at your disposal. We can fly together. I'll clear my schedule so we can spend time in Philadelphia. I'll enjoy seeing your parents again."

"You're so overworked now. I can handle traveling alone."

Giuseppe yawned loudly, getting their attention.

Matteo stood. "Grandfather, you're tired. I'll ring for your nurse." He looked down at Chloe. "We will finish this conversation in our suite."

CHAPTER 18

The tap of their shoes on the marble marked each apprehensive step Chloe took with Matteo to their quarters. The tightness around his mouth told her she'd angered him by announcing she planned to leave soon.

When they got to their rooms, he opened the door and waved her in. Ignoring him and her own rapidly beating heart, she started removing her earrings and rings, depositing them on the dresser top.

He threw his jacket and tie on a chair. Chloe folded her arms across her chest and faced him, filling her lungs with air, steeling herself. "I know you're angry, but we never settled on a timeline and I have to get home."

"You threw that at me with no warning." He rubbed the back of his neck. "Why are you going now? Giuseppe still needs you. He's improved since you came back."

Sighing, she sank onto the bed, drew in a breath, held it for a heartbeat. "He seems better. I told you how energetic he was the other day at the gallery. I don't like to think if I go now, it might be the last time I see him. But I agreed to come here and pretend we've reunited, for your grandfather. We've done that. He believes it and he understands I have a business to run. Maybe I can come back after I take care of things at home. I've kept my end of the bargain. I expect you to keep yours. You have the divorce papers. Sign them, and I'll be gone."

But not out of your life, not with two children between us.

He paced the room, then turned to her. "Damn if I'll allow you to leave now." Anger colored his voice.

Chloe jumped up. "You don't get to *allow* me to do anything. You never did."

He stood inches from her, his eyes sparking gold fire. "It's the boyfriend, isn't it? You're so anxious to go back to him, you'd desert Grandfather."

"Don't throw that guilt trip on me. I won't fall for it, not anymore." Narrowing her eyes, she glared at him, refusing to move.

He let loose a string of Italian curses.

"No need to curse. We can discuss this like adults."

"God help me." He pulled her to him. His mouth descended on hers in a hard, hungry kiss that slammed the breath out of her. His ravenous lips feasted on her, drawing her into his fire.

His fierce kiss cajoled and seduced, shattering the shell of loneliness around her heart. Her spirit yearned for the intimacy they'd once shared. His scent of sandalwood filled her. Desire wrestled with reason. Like a starving woman, she released a desperate whimper and tangled her fingers in his hair. His erection, hard and hot, pressed against her stomach.

Her mind tumbled back three years when their love was ferocious in its intensity. She knew his touch and the feel of his smooth skin against hers. Her body desired him. Her soul craved him. With an aching need, she opened her mouth, inviting his possession.

His tongue swept into her mouth.

They fell together on the bed. He slanted his lips over hers again and again. His hand slid inside her shirt and trailed a hot path to her chest. Her nipples tightened. When he took one of her breasts in his hand, she arched her back, her low cries urging him to give her more.

He left her mouth to tenderly kiss her neck, her collarbone, the curve of her shoulder. Boneless, she melted into the mattress. He raised himself and pulled her shirt up. She lifted her arms to help him remove the thin cotton. Reaching behind her, he unhooked her bra and threw the lacy garment aside.

Sitting back on his haunches, he stared down at her with an expression of wonder. "I've never forgotten you, your soft skin, your taste. You've been in my dreams for so long. I never thought to possess you again."

The power of his words stoked longing and love deep inside her. "I've never forgotten you, either."

His skin stretched taut over his high cheekbones as his hot, wicked gaze caressed her. With exquisite care, he removed her sandals and slid her Capris down her body, discarding both, until she lay before him clad only in a tiny pair of lace panties and the silver necklace with the flower motif pendant. She'd put it on earlier and couldn't explain why.

He reached out to touch the pendant. "I can still see you at that vendor stand trying to negotiate with the merchant for this."

"And you came to my rescue."

"I will always come to your rescue, cara mia."

A wet pool of arousal rushed to her lower abdomen. She held her arms out to him and released his name on a breathless sigh.

Pushing aside her panties, he plunged two fingers inside her. She moaned her pleasure at the unexpected and sensuous invasion. He explored and played until she was a quivering mass of want. His mouth and tongue followed where his fingers stroked, pushing her to the edge.

Her orgasm built, twisting flames consuming her. Her fingers bit into the flesh of his shoulders as she exploded, erupting in a crescendo of dazzling fire to rival Vesuvius. Her cries filled the room.

He released her and stared down at her. His eyes smoldered. Without words, he told her she belonged to him.

He undressed quickly and stood before her, Adonis come to life. A dusting of dark hair covered the defined muscles of his broad chest. She drank in his slim hips and long, beautifully shaped legs. She reached out and traced the hard length of his erection with her fingers. He threw back his head and groaned, the sound guttural and raw.

The mattress dipped as he sank onto the bed. Bracing his weight on his forearms, he settled himself over her. He kissed her waiting lips, claiming her. She linked her arms around his neck, reveling in his heat, his passion, her love for him.

He began a slow, careful exploration of her body, his mouth following where his hands touched. She quivered beneath him. Her skin tingled where he touched. Strangled whimpers rose from her throat. With skill and tenderness, he brought her body to life.

He massaged her swollen breasts, and suckled one hard nipple, then the other, swirling his tongue over and over her nipples until she cried out with another shattering orgasm. He looked at her, his mouth tilted in a triumphant smile.

He continued his sensual assault, licking and kissing her midriff and the flesh of her stomach. Trembling, she opened her legs, welcoming him to take her fully. He entered her easily, sinking into her.

"Chloe." His raw, desperate voice fueled her desire.

He moved inside her, slowly at first, driving her to arch her hips, taking him deeper. She surrendered to his possession. He rode her faster and harder. She met his every thrust.

Her orgasm burst around her. She dug her fingernails into the firm skin of his back.

He cried out and stiffened with his own climax.

They held each other, only the sheen of sweat separating them. Finally, he rolled off her and gathered her to him, holding her close. He kissed her temple with tenderness, like he'd done so many times before.

She was where she belonged.

CHAPTER 19

Light streaming through the windows woke Matteo. He stirred and sighed with contentment. The woman sleeping beside him, her arm draped over his chest, calmed the beast in his soul, the sad beast with the empty heart only Chloe could fill. He turned slightly to watch her peaceful face in slumber. Her brown hair with the auburn highlights spilled over the pillow. Her thick, dark lashes fanned over the smoothness of her sun-kissed face. He'd never known anyone so beautiful in every way.

Careful not to wake her, he lay on his back and folded his arms beneath his head to stare at the ceiling. Sunlight touched the small crystal chandelier hanging from an ornate medallion. Prisms of light reflected off the walls, mirroring the brightness Chloe brought to him.

He needed to convince her to give them another chance, needed to keep her by his side. She had a thriving business to run. He got that. They could figure out a way to live on two continents and keep their marriage alive.

His stomach clenched. In his conceit, he assumed she still loved him. She'd never said the words. She made love with the passion, excitement, and enthusiasm she'd always possessed, but that didn't mean she loved him.

She had a lover back in Philadelphia.

He had to make her forget that other guy, to want him, Matteo, and only him. Determination tensed his muscles. He turned to her and gathered her to him. Her scent of jasmine teased him. He kissed her full lips and the curve of her jaw.

She sighed and tangled her fingers in his hair. "I want to wake up like this every morning," she whispered.

He lifted his head and looked into her passion-glazed gray eyes. "You can."

Surprise flitted across her face. He gave her no time to respond, but turned his attention to pleasing her. When he nuzzled her deep cleavage, he was rewarded by her small cry of pleasure. She arched her hips, her breathing shallow.

He lay her on her back, the better to sample the banquet of sensuousness she presented to him. With his mouth and hands, he feasted on the lavish slopes of her body, kissing her stomach, her thighs. He stroked the sensitive nub between her legs.

"Matteo. Please."

Her needy cries filled the room.

In one fluid motion, he rolled onto his back and pulled her atop him. "Fuck me."

"Yes."

He put his hands around her waist and lifted her.

Passion constricted her face, and she sank down until he filled her completely. She moved over him slowly at first, a sensual goddess who'd put him under her spell. He cupped and massaged her full breasts and sucked her hard nipples. Throwing back her head, she rode him fast and hard.

He gripped her hips. "Mine."

She cried out with the force of her climax. His ripped through him. Panting, she lay on top of him. He held her tight, never wanting to let go.

Finally, she slid off him and he brought the covers up over them, cocooning them in love. She nestled against his chest and kissed his throat.

"Wow!" she said. "After last night and now. Just wow!"

Chuckling, he said, "You don't think we're finished yet, do you?"

She smiled and stroked his face. "I should hope not." Her expression grew serious. "Matteo, we didn't use protection."

"Don't worry. I haven't been with anyone since you left."

Her eyes widened. "You haven't? I saw pictures of you with other women."

He brushed his knuckles against her cheek. "I couldn't. I wanted only you."

"I haven't been with anyone else either."

Surprise, joy, and a dollop of male pride rushed through him, and he kissed her waiting lips.

She pulled gently away. "What if I get pregnant?"

"We're married. I want a child with you."

Alarm flashed in her eyes, surprising him.

"What's wrong, cara mia?"

"Nothing." Her gaze met his. "Make love to me again."

"Slow this time. We have all morning."

CHAPTER 20

Clad in her silk robe, Chloe sat at the vanity and smoothed a brush down her hair. She started to pin it up, but Matteo, dressed in an untucked gray shirt and jeans, stood behind her and touched her hand, stopping her.

"Keep your hair down. I like it that way." Their eyes met in the mirror.

"I planned to help Francesca today. I want to look professional."

"I want you to look sexy for me." He slid his hand beneath her robe to massage her breast. "I want you again."

His touch fueled new desire in her and brought a smile to her lips. "Again? After what we did in bed, and in the shower just now, you want more?"

"I can never get enough of you."

Reality slammed into her, black paint thrown against the brightness of her happiness. She stood slowly. "I need to get dressed, then we must talk, really talk."

He pulled her to him. “I want to try again, Chloe. I know there are issues we’ve never worked out, but I want another chance.”

She grabbed his hand and brought it to her mouth to kiss his palm tenderly. “There’s something I must tell you that might change everything.”

He closed his eyes. When he opened them, sadness and resignation darkened their depths. “You love another man.”

“Oh, no. That’s not it, but what I….” She let the words drop. The day of reckoning was here. She could no longer put off the inevitable, what she should have done long ago. Anxiety strode with her to the dressing room.

Wearing a green T-shirt and white capris, her feet in flat sandals, she came into the bedroom to find Matteo waiting, his face solemn.

“I rang for coffee and pastries,” he said. “Let’s go to the patio. When the food gets here, we’ll eat, then we’ll talk.”

They finished breakfast quickly. She barely tasted the delicate pastries or the strong coffee. Chloe poured them each more coffee, and with her hands wrapped around the mug, she sat back, her attention on Matteo sitting across from her.

She sipped her drink and set down the cup, meeting his eyes. “Where did we go wrong? We were so in love. Maybe we needed a longer courtship to work things out. I’ve always been independent, but this villa, your noble family, your mother, you, intimidated me, a Philadelphia woman from a working-class family. I was so anxious to please everyone, especially you, things between us spiraled out of control.”

"Our love flashed so quickly and so passionately, neither of us stopped to take a breath."

She smiled and picked up her coffee, finishing it. "True." Setting the empty cup on the table, she pushed it away.

He looked out toward the gardens before locking gazes with her again. "I was egotistical and spoiled, too sure of myself and my appeal." Shaking his head, he chuckled. "I thought I could charm you into doing whatever I wanted, be whatever I wanted. I couldn't accept you wouldn't blindly believe everything I told you, that you'd let Mama and Ingrid and others put doubts in your mind."

"Yes, you were full of yourself, confident, and these were things that attracted me to you. But you shrugged off the lies about you as nothing. And you didn't stand up for me. That hurt more than anything."

"I didn't see the need to defend myself or protect you, and I didn't understand what the lies did to you, to us. I thought you understood I had to act a certain way for the public, but that I loved you unconditionally." He put his hand over hers on the table. "I talked to Mama back then and asked her to be kinder to you. I'm sorry she wasn't and that I wasn't stronger with her."

"Your mother has been friendlier to me lately. There's hope for her and me." Chloe leaned forward. "When I confronted you with the rumors about your infidelity, you said you didn't owe me an explanation for anything. As the wife of a DiMarco, I should have unshakable faith in you. I needed you to assure me of your love, to swear you weren't cheating on me."

"And I expected you to trust me completely."

Old, simmering rage propelled her to stand. "Would it have killed you to give me what I wanted?"

He stood too and grabbed her hands, holding them in his large ones. "Please, no anger. We will work this out. Yes, I should have recognized your need, but my hurt that you would think I'd cheat on you, that you didn't understand I never looked at another woman from the time I saw you at Piazza del Duomo, blinded me. My pride let you walk away, the worst mistake of my life."

Tears stung her eyes. "When you didn't follow me, I figured you didn't love me anymore, perhaps never did, and had grown tired of me. I was something new to you, different from the models and royals you dated."

He gathered her into his embrace. "I will never grow tired of you, cara mia. I appreciated how real you were, how unlike the women I'd been used to." He kissed her temple and the tip of her nose, then pushed her gently away. He brushed hair back from her face with exquisite tenderness. "Forgive me, Chloe."

"I forgive you. We were both at fault. Perhaps we needed this time away from each other to better understand our relationship. And to grow. Forgive me for not having faith in you."

His smile lit his eyes. "Of course, I forgive you. Does this mean you'll stay with me, give our marriage another chance?"

She bit down on her lip and freed herself from him. Rubbing her arms, she strode to the railing and looked down to the lush, green gardens and the turquoise sea below.

"Chloe? What is it?"

Her heart pounded, the sound echoing in her ears. She turned to him.

"You'd better sit. I hope you'll forgive me after what I'm about to tell you."

CHAPTER 21

Frowning, he sank into his chair, sitting on the edge, his body rigid. "This sounds serious. What could you possibly do I wouldn't forgive?"

She wrapped her arms around her waist and leaned on the railing, facing him. The hard iron dug into her back, the slight pain penance for her cowardice and deceit. She blew out a breath and dived in. "I left here two years ago pregnant with twins."

He jerked his head back. "What?" He jumped up. In two strides, he stood in front of her. His eyes flashed uncertainty and surprise. "We have children?"

Words froze and she nodded.

He let loose a volley of curses in Italian, and fury clouded his eyes. "Two children, and you never told me?"

"I'm sorry."

"Sorry? You're *sorry* you kept me from my children?" He tunneled fingers through his hair and stepped back. "What kind of cruelty is this?"

"I was afraid if you knew, I'd lose them."

"You think I would take your children from you?"

The quietness of his tone frightened her. She'd rather he raised his voice.

"I was afraid Valentina would take them."

"Mama take our kids?"

"I overheard her talking to a friend. She said something about keeping any children we have here, and stopping me from taking them to the U.S. She said she wanted to raise them the way a noble DiMarco deserved. I feared she'd fight for custody. Your family has connections in the judicial system."

Matteo cursed again and paced the patio.

Chloe pressed a palm to her shaking stomach. Her parents were right. She should have told him when she knew she was pregnant.

He whirled to face her. "Why didn't you tell me this? You know Mama. She likes to talk big, but she wouldn't take your children, our children. I wouldn't let her."

"I have no excuse except my hormones were going crazy, and I thought the rumors you'd been unfaithful were true. I didn't believe I could handle being pregnant while dealing with your mother and your infidelities. Even so, I wanted to tell you, that day you came back from Paris, but we had the fight about Ingrid and you refused to discuss anything with me. You walked out on me and didn't spend the night in our room. I took that to mean you didn't care about me, and if you didn't care for me, our children and I would be burdens to you. If I told you about the pregnancy, you'd do the *right* thing and stay with me for the sake of the children. I wanted you to *want* to be with me."

He moved until only inches separated them. "That's rubbish about our fight over Ingrid. You didn't try very hard to tell me. Instead, you ran away, leaving me with a note that said nothing. You lied to me for two years, never telling me about the children. My children. What you did was cowardly, and not like the woman I married."

"I wanted to protect the babies I carried." She twisted the hem of her T-shirt between her fingers before meeting his stormy eyes again. "I believed you'd follow me. Then I could tell you about my pregnancy, away from Valentina and this place where I felt intimidated, meeting on my home turf as it were. I knew if you came after me, it would mean you loved me, but you didn't come and you never bothered to contact me. I waited all through my pregnancy for you, and then it seemed the longer I went without telling you, the harder it became."

"I didn't contact you because my heart was too devastated. It took a long time to get my head on straight after you left. You could have called me at any time."

"But if I called you to tell you about the children, and you asked me to come back, it would be because you felt a sense of obligation, not that you loved and wanted me. Or that you wanted our children."

"Madone!" He rubbed a hand over his hair. "This is all nonsense."

He paced the length of the patio again, then whirled to face her. "What are their names?"

"Giuseppe and Sofia, after your grandparents. We call them by their American names, Joey and Sofie."

Matteo's face drained of color. "A boy and a girl?"

"Yes."

"I demand to see them."

"Of course."

Hurt slanted across his face. "When did you plan to tell me, or did you figure to keep them from me forever?"

She clutched her hands at her sides to stop their shaking. "I planned to tell you before I left here."

"After I signed the divorce papers?"

At his narrowed eyes and soft voice, she could only nod.

"You would have me sign divorce papers before you told me about my children? My children. Why did you make love with me? Was that part of your game? Did you think you would soften me up so I would forgive what you've done?"

"No, Matteo. No. I made love with you because I wanted to. I love you."

"You're too late with words of love."

He turned on his heel and headed toward the door, but before he strode out, he looked back at her. "You are not the woman I thought you were."

* * *

SOBS ERUPTED FROM CHLOE. She collapsed on the patio floor, her arms wrapped around her stomach. Her whole body shook as huge, gulping cries overtook her.

Matteo would never forgive her. He hated her.

Any chance to repair their marriage dissolved into the sunny Italian sky.

He needed his children, and they needed him.

Her tears flowed freely, cleansing ones she'd been

unable to shed the past two years. She scooted over, leaned against the railing, and let her anxieties and mistakes pour out, a torrent that finally subsided, leaving her exhausted. Shame rushed through her. Matteo was right. She'd been cowardly. Quietness settled around her, mocking the turmoil of her life.

* * *

RED-HOT RAGE and deep pain pushed Matteo through the villa, his shoes slapping on the marble floors, echoing his conflict and wrath. He strode out the side door to the garage where Nunzio was shining the Maserati.

"Away!" Matteo shouted. "I need the car."

Nunzio back-pedaled away.

Matteo slid into the car and drove out, too fast. The Maserati fish-tailed on the driveway. He took deep breaths. He had to control his fury. If he crashed, he might never see his children.

Twins. A boy and a girl. He gripped the steering wheel as he headed away from the palazzo. Chloe lied to him for two years. Worse than lies. Hid his children from him in the ultimate betrayal.

She'd changed. He didn't know if he could ever forgive her.

Traffic was light. He shifted gears and sped up, needing the revving sound of the engine to soothe his confusion and hurt.

How could she do this to him? Had she trusted him so little?

In Ravello, he parked and walked to the piazza. As if

his body were a separate entity, he found himself in front of the Cathedral of Ravello, where he and Chloe were married. He mounted the steps and opened the heavy bronze doors.

The dim, cool interior of the ornate medieval church did little to calm him. A few people sat in pews. He went to a pew at the back and slipped in.

His mind jumbled with thoughts, all vying for attention. Chloe's deceit. The twins. The fierce, passionate lovemaking last night and this morning. He cursed himself for every kind of fool.

His anger competed with a sliver of joy. Children, a boy and a girl. Children to teach the ways of the world, to introduce to their heritage, to love them, and worry over them. He'd always wanted a family with Chloe, the love of his life.

He wondered if they looked like him or Chloe or a combination of both. He needed to see them, hug them, claim them. He raised his gaze to the large crucifix hanging at the altar. "God, tell me what to do."

He sat for an hour, inhaling the scents of incense and wood. No answer came from God, but Matteo found peace. And determination to make things right.

CHAPTER 22

Chloe moved in a daze. She needed to talk to Giuseppe, to tell him about the twins. Being with him always calmed her. She hoped he'd understand why she kept the children from him and Matteo.

Dread marched with her to the elderly man's quarters. His nurse answered her knock and waved Chloe in. Smiling, she pointed to the patio where Giuseppe sat in his wheelchair. The nurse left the room, closing the door quietly behind her.

Drawing relaxing breaths, Chloe went to Giuseppe. He looked up when she stepped out.

"What is wrong, Chloe? Sadness clouds your face." He gestured to a chair across the table from him. "Sit and pour yourself some coffee."

Chloe did as he said, her hands shaking as she poured. She sipped the strong brew, needing the caffeine to strengthen her resolve. Gripping the cup, she met his eyes.

"I have something to tell you, something I should have told Matteo and you a long time ago."

His gentle brown eyes held love. "Of course. You look scared. Don't be. Whatever it is, I will accept."

Her tears flowed freely again. She set down her mug and rubbed away the wetness on her face. "When I left here two years ago, I was pregnant with twins. Matteo and I have a boy and a girl."

He dropped the coffee cup he held. It hit the floor and shattered, spreading shards of glass on the flagstone, the fragments mirroring her crushed life.

"You and Matteo have children?" he finally said.

"Yes. I'm so sorry I kept them from you both."

"Does my grandson know?"

"I told him a little while ago. He stormed out. I think he hates me."

"He loves you. My grandson is a kind man, and a smart one. He will come to his senses." Giuseppe leaned forward and touched her hand. "Why did you not tell us before this?"

Chloe released a long sigh. "I foolishly thought Valentina would take custody of them."

He moved back in his chair. "My daughter-in-law may be haughty and put on airs but she would never take your children away."

"I was young and foolish. I thought Matteo had taken lovers, that he didn't love me. I figured if I left, he'd follow me and prove his love. Then I would tell him. He never came. The longer I went without telling him, the harder it became. I'm sorry. I shouldn't have done it."

"You made a mistake. We all make mistakes."

"Thank you for understanding."

"What are their names?" he asked with gentleness.

"Giuseppe and Sofia."

His eyes glistened. "Thank you for that."

He glanced away, before meeting her gaze again with haunted eyes.

"I, too, have done a wrong to you and my grandson."

"Wrong?"

"I am not sick."

Her mind played tricks on her. She could swear he said he wasn't sick.

"I'm as healthy as a person my age can be," he continued. "My doctor says I may live to 100, or longer."

"But—but, why? I mean, I'm glad you're well, but I don't understand."

"My grandson has suffered since you left. He loves you and needs you. Whenever I tried to talk about you, he'd cut me off. I had to do something extreme to bring you together, so I came up with this little deceit."

Irritation tightened her chest, but she tamped it down. "It's more than little, Giuseppe, but what I did was worse. I'm guilty of a very big lie of omission that is hurtful to you and Matteo, two people I love very much."

He waved a hand. "We've both done wrong, but we will fix it."

"I'm not sure we can fix what's between Matteo and me. What made you play this charade?"

"I saw my grandson's stubbornness when he received the divorce papers and knew he'd sign them and never see you again. I had to give him a reason to go to you."

"Why were you sure I still loved him? What if I had another man in my life?"

He smiled. "I saw pictures on the internet of you and a young man at a social function in Philadelphia. You looked comfortable together. I had to work fast. You and Matteo have a love for each other that lights up a room. Anyone can see the depth of your feelings. That kind of love doesn't easily die. It was the same between my Sofia and me."

"I do love him," she said quietly.

"Tell him. You will figure things out."

She shook her head. "I told him, but it doesn't make any difference. You didn't see his face when he walked out. It's too late. This morning, I booked airfare to Philadelphia. My babies need me. And I need them."

"Don't leave yet. Talk to Matteo. You will resolve this."

"Distance will give us both time to settle down. We can't talk with so much emotion and hurt between us. He wants to see the children, and it's his right. They deserve to see their father, too."

She wiped away an errant tear trailing down her face.

"Give Matteo a chance, Chloe. His love for you is strong. Please stay here and work this out with him."

"I may have killed whatever love he has for me." She stood and bent to kiss Giuseppe on the cheek. "I have to pack. My flight is scheduled late tomorrow night. I'll come say goodbye before I leave. I'm happy you're not ill, but a little disturbed you lied to us."

"I want to meet my great-grandchildren."

"Of course."

"How will you travel to the airport in Rome?"

"I'll hire a car."

He sighed. "If I can't keep you from going, at least let Nunzio drive you."

"Thank you. I love you."

Blinded by tears, Chloe fled.

CHAPTER 23

Matteo didn't come back that night. Restless, Chloe tossed and turned, finally going to the chaise and listening for his footsteps, for the door opening. Near dawn, she gave up the fight and rose.

Upset and needing to be alone, Chloe had stayed to herself the day before. She wondered where Matteo spent the night. Fearing something had happened to him, she'd called his cell several times. It went straight to voicemail. The DiMarco's kept an apartment in Ravello. Maybe he slept there.

She put on her robe, tying the belt tightly as if she could rein in her worries, and headed to the kitchen to make coffee. The quiet of the villa pressed against her, reflecting her sadness. Her slippers shuffled on the marble floors. She might never see this beautiful place again. Coffee made, she took a tray with a carafe and cups back to her suite. She sat on her patio sipping her drink, her thoughts chaotic and distressed. Streaks of pinks and purples traced across the brightening sky. A new day.

Home and her babies beckoned. Hope sprang up in her that Matteo would come to Philadelphia after her this time, that they'd work things out between them, be a family. Maybe she should take Giuseppe's advice and stay, talk to Matteo.

* * *

NUNZIO STORED Chloe's luggage in the limo and agreed to wait for her near the gallery, where she planned to say goodbye to Francesca. She hurried to Giuseppe's quarters and knocked on the door, surprised when he answered.

"Buongiorno, Giuseppe. Are you alone? Where's your nurse?"

"She is no longer needed. Please come in, Chloe."

She slipped into the room and he closed the door. She scanned the elderly man. "You look like the Giuseppe I remember, straight and tall, and well-dressed as only you Italians can manage."

"It is good to be myself. Please accept my apologies again for the lies I told you and Matteo."

"I could never be angry with you, Grandfather. I don't like dishonesty, but I understand why you did this. I'm guilty of my own sins."

"Let's sit." He gestured to the sitting room. "Enjoy some coffee and sandwiches. You have a long drive to Rome so you should eat before you go."

They sat across from each other at the small table. Chloe poured them each coffee and filled plates with Lucia's delicious sandwiches. They ate in silence. Finished, she pushed aside her plate and cup and met the elderly man's eyes.

"I have a question," she said.

"I will answer anything you want to know."

"Were your doctor and nurse in on your little charade?"

"No. My doctor would never have sanctioned something like that. I hired the nurse from an agency. She had no idea."

"You sure fooled us."

"Have you spoken to Matteo?"

She shook her head. "He didn't come home last night. I called his cell phone several times but it went straight to voicemail. I hope he's okay."

Giuseppe patted her hand across the table. "Perhaps he spent the night at our apartment in Ravello."

"I thought that might be the case." She stood, and Giuseppe stood with her. "I need to say goodbye to Francesca before I leave. Nunzio is waiting to drive me to Rome."

"It's not too late for you to change your mind and stay. Talk to Matteo."

Her eyes wet, she hugged the old man. "I need to go. I've been away from the children too long. I'll think of you every day, Grandfather. I can leave knowing your health is good."

He drew away and held her at arms' length, his eyes soft with love. "We will see each other again soon. Perhaps I'll fly to Philadelphia to meet my great-grandchildren."

"Please do. I'll tell them all about you."

They hugged again, then Chloe left before she became a sobbing mess.

The house was still with no one around when she headed outside. She hadn't seen Valentina or Ingrid for several days.

She walked down the drive leading to the gallery. Nunzio stood near the limo, waiting. He tipped his cap to her.

Francesca, in her small Fiat, drove up and waved to Chloe. She parked and approached Chloe smiling.

"Ciao, Chloe. I didn't expect you today," Francesca said.

"I came to say goodbye."

Francesca's eyes widened. "Goodbye? Why?"

"I have to go back to Philadelphia. My business needs me." She didn't mention the children. That would take too much explaining, and her emotions were too raw. She hated goodbyes. She wanted to get into the car and ride away.

"You will be back, no?" Francesca asked.

"I'm sure I will. Come, give me a hug."

The women embraced.

Chloe touched Francesca's arm. "Take care of yourself and that husband of yours." She turned and walked to the waiting car that would take her from the man she loved.

Doubts plagued her as the car headed out. She didn't know if she was doing the right thing, running away.

They entered the highway and headed toward Naples. Chloe leaned forward and touched Nunzio on the shoulder. "Nunzio, turn around please. Take me back home. To Ravello."

CHAPTER 24

Matteo pulled his car into the circular drive in front of the villa, cut the engine, and climbed out. Police sirens coming closer disturbed the early afternoon quiet.

The front door opened and Giuseppe stepped out, his face tight with worry. The old man, dressed in his usual elegant way, as he'd done before he took sick, walked with quick steps despite his cane.

"Grandfather, you're not in your wheelchair."

Giuseppe waved him off. "Later. Francesca called. She was too upset to talk. Something has happened at the gallery."

The elderly man kept moving. Matteo hurriedly followed and touched Giuseppe's arm, stopping him. Giuseppe turned to face him.

"Tell me first why you're using your cane and not your wheelchair."

His grandfather sighed. "I'm not sick. It was a deceit to bring you and Chloe together."

"What?"

"I'm sorry. I apologized to Chloe yesterday. I thought if I were dying, you and she would reconcile. I know you love each other, but you are both stubborn. I had to do something."

Matteo brushed his hand over his hair, trying to rein in his conflicting emotions of shock and anger. "Grandfather, I can't believe you did this. What were you thinking?"

"I brought you together, didn't I?"

"That's not the point. You lied and worried us for nothing. How is Chloe taking this? I need to talk to her."

"She's not here." Giuseppe kept walking—with Matteo on his heels.

"Where is she? Is she all right?"

"She's fine. Now, let's see what has upset Francesca."

Two police cars, lights flashing, raced down the gallery driveway. Matteo and Giuseppe looked at each other and quickened their pace.

A distraught Francesca was wringing her hands and pacing outside the building.

The police parked their cars and alighted from the vehicles at the same time Matteo and Giuseppe reached Francesca.

"What happened?" Matteo asked her.

She swung her attention to the police, then to him. "Oh, Signore DiMarco. It's terrible, just terrible." Big gulping sobs escaped her, and tears streaked her face.

"What happened, child?" Giuseppe asked.

"The blue Murano vase. It's gone."

"Gone?" Matteo brushed past her to enter the gallery. The case that held the expensive vase was empty. He examined the case. It was undamaged. He walked back outside.

"What is the problem, signora?" a policeman asked Francesca.

"A very expensive vase is missing," she said through sobs.

Notebook in hand, the cop asked for her name, then turned to Matteo. "What is your name please? Could we have a description of the missing item."

Matteo gave them the information they requested. "We have photos of the vase in some books in the gift shop."

"That would be most helpful, Signore DiMarco. Please show us where the vase was when it went missing."

Matteo, Francesca and Giuseppe, along with the cops, trooped into the gallery.

"Who discovered the alleged theft?" the cop with the notebook asked.

"I did." Francesca tearfully recounted that when she entered the gallery for the start of her day, she found the vase gone, the case unlocked. Whoever took it must have known the security code and have a key to the gallery and case. The alarm didn't trip. She insisted she'd activated the security system when she closed up the evening before, and it was still on this morning when she disarmed it. Someone had to have turned it off and back on.

"The alarm didn't ring when the vase was stolen?" one of the cops asked.

She rubbed tears from her face and shook her head. "If

the alarm goes off, the security company gets notification and sends the police. I called the company. They had no notice of a break-in. Then I called the police."

One of the policemen turned to Matteo. "Would you have heard the alarm in the house?"

"No. It's silent."

Francesca took a tissue out of her purse and blew her nose, swinging her attention between Matteo and Giuseppe. "I am so sorry. This is all my fault."

"How is it your fault, my dear?" Giuseppe asked.

"I never changed the security code Chloe set up two years ago. She told me I should change it, but I've been so busy."

"Who has this code?" The officer held his pen over his notebook.

Francesca wadded her tissue in her hand. "I do. Also, Chloe, Signora DiMarco. And Signori Matteo and Giuseppe DiMarco, and Signora Valentina DiMarco."

"Why does my mother have the code?" Matteo asked. "There's no reason for her to have it."

"She came to me a few weeks ago and asked for it. She said she and Ingrid wanted to give a private tour to some friends." Francesca bit her lip. "I am so sorry if I was wrong to give it to her."

Matteo moved away from the group, his thoughts chaotic. His instincts screamed his mother and Ingrid had something to do with the missing vase. Why would they steal it? To sell? That made no sense, at least for his mother. Whoever stole the valuable item could face prison time. Neither woman would risk that. Like the sun bursting through clouds, a thought formed. They'd tried to hurt Chloe before. They may have figured a way to blame her for the theft. He couldn't believe they'd be so cruel, or so stupid. Yet, doubts persisted. If that was their game, it wouldn't work. He'd defend Chloe with all he had.

After much soul-searching last night, he realized Chloe made the decision she had about the children to protect them. As a mother, her children came first. He also understood her doubts about him, doubts he'd done nothing to alleviate. He hadn't fought for Chloe, for their marriage. He vowed to spend his life making it up to her.

"Signore DiMarco, please."

The officer's voice cut through Matteo's self-recriminations. "Yes?"

"We need to question all who have the security code. Could you be so kind as to ask the others to make themselves available?"

He nodded. "My wife isn't here." He gave his grandfather a pointed look. "Where is she?"

"She's on her way to Rome, then to Philadelphia. I will explain later." He turned to the cops. "Why would I steal my own vase?"

The policeman with the notebook clicked it shut and included all of them in his gaze. "Everyone who has that security code is suspect. I will question each of you individually."

The cop's voice seemed to come from far away. Matteo's head spun. Chloe left him again? He couldn't let her go like he did the last time. He had to convince her of his love, beg her to stay with him and work out their problems. He pulled out his phone and looked at Giuseppe. "When did she leave?"

"Not long ago. You might have passed the limo on your way here."

Matteo punched in Chloe's number as he strode quickly outside.

The phone rang several times, and he feared she wouldn't answer. Finally, her hesitant voice came on the line.

"Matteo? Are you okay? I worried when you didn't come home last night."

"I'm fine. Please come back to me. Don't leave. I need you and love you. We'll work things out."

"We just pulled up to the villa."

"You're here?"

"I couldn't run away a second time. I love you."

He disconnected the call and raced to the front of the palazzo to find Chloe climbing out of the limo, aided by Nunzio.

He ran to her and gathered her into his arms, holding her close, never wanting to let her go.

"Don't ever leave me again," he whispered.

"I won't. I realized I was being a coward again. I'm here to stay."

He pulled away and kissed her tenderly on the lips.

Nunzio, a grin on his face, hauled Chloe's luggage from the trunk.

Matteo stared at the suitcases, and he knew.

"Chloe, open your large bag."

Her forehead creased. "Why?"

"Do it. You'll see."

She unzipped the bag. “What’s this large lump?” She dug through some clothes and pulled out the Murano vase. Holding it, she stood, her confused gaze meeting Matteo’s. “What’s this doing here?”

“I think I know.” He cupped her elbow. “Come with me.”

CHAPTER 25

Chloe's mind couldn't quite grasp what had happened. The expensive vase in her suitcase? Questions tripped over each other in her head. She gasped at the police cars parked in front of the gallery. "What's going on?" she asked Matteo.

"I'll explain later. Let's get this vase back where it belongs."

Francesca's face broke into a huge grin when she saw them enter the gallery with the vase. She ran up to them. "You found it! Where?"

"I'll tell you later," Matteo said.

They put the Murano in its case. Matteo assured the police the theft was a family matter they'd handle. The police left, and Matteo explained to Giuseppe and Francesca that the stolen item was in Chloe's luggage. A relieved, but still confused, Francesca opened the gallery for the day, while Matteo, Giuseppe, and Chloe headed to the house.

Federico opened the door for them as they approached.

"Federico, have my mother and Ingrid meet me in my office," Matteo said.

"They are not here, Signore. They left for Ravello early this morning, in Signora Ingrid's car."

Matteo chuckled. "I have a good idea why they left." He nodded to Federico. "Let me know when they come back."

"Very well."

Chloe grabbed Matteo's hand. "Are you going to tell me what's happening? Did they put the vase in my luggage?"

"I'm certain they did."

"I need to rest after this excitement," Giuseppe said. "I can't believe Valentina and Ingrid would be so cruel. How did they think to get away with this?"

"Apparently, they didn't think it out." Matteo turned to Chloe. "Let's go up to our room and I'll explain everything."

Giuseppe led the way upstairs. He headed to his quarters while Chloe and Matteo went to theirs.

When they got into their suite, Chloe turned to Matteo. "Please, tell me what's going on."

He pulled her to him. "First, we need to talk about us." He cupped her face and looked into her eyes. "Whatever problems we have, we'll resolve together. I never want to be separated from you again. I did a lot of thinking, and I finally realize I didn't give you the support you needed, that I took you and your love for granted. Forgive me for not understanding what you went through, for not defending you or our marriage."

She saw love and truth in the golden depths of his eyes. "I forgive you. I love you. Do you forgive me for not telling you about the children?"

"I'll forgive you anything. I recognize why you kept them from me. I don't like it, but I understand. Neither of us had enough faith in the other. That changes now."

"I'd been cowardly that first time, running away. I should have stayed and made you talk to me. I won't ever leave you."

"I love you, Chloe."

"I love you, Matteo."

He took her waiting lips in a whisper-soft kiss that promised a lifetime of love.

* * *

VALENTINA AND INGRID came back to the palazzo later that afternoon. Heaviness tempered the happiness in Matteo's heart. He had an unpleasant task ahead, but he and Chloe were together, and with love and understanding, would be forever. Voices from the hall reached him as he sat waiting at the small table in his office, a mug of coffee in front of him. His mother and Ingrid, stormy expressions on their faces, marched in.

"Why was it necessary to demand we come see you?" his mother asked. "We are tired from a long day of shopping."

He gestured to two of the chairs around the table. "Sit, Mama, Ingrid."

"You have no right to order me—."

"I have every right, Mama. Now, sit."

The women, confusion on their faces, sank onto the chairs.

He sipped his coffee, letting their curiosity brew for a while. Finally, he slammed his empty mug on the table, causing the women to jump. "No games. Answers. Honest ones. The police were here earlier. Someone stole the Murano vase. I believe you are both guilty."

His mother swore, then turned accusing eyes to Ingrid. "You stole it? After I told you the plan was off?"

Ingrid widened her blue eyes and turned to Matteo. "I did not steal the vase. Valentina did. It was her idea."

Valentina stood up with enough force to topple her chair. "Liar!" She looked at her son. "I did not do it."

"Mama, tell me what plan was off."

She righted her chair and lowered herself onto it. Tears streamed down her face. "Forgive me, son." She turned a dark look to Ingrid.

The blonde started to rise.

"Sit down, Ingrid," he said.

She sat slowly, fear on her face.

"Continue, Mama."

His mother folded her hands tightly together on the table. "Ingrid and I wanted Chloe gone. We planned to steal the vase and have Chloe take the blame. If she went to prison for theft, you'd be free to divorce her and marry someone worthy of a DiMarco." She laughed, a sound with no mirth. "Ingrid thought you'd marry her if Chloe was out of your life. I let her believe that so she'd help me chase your wife away."

Ingrid sputtered. "You lied to me!"

"Quiet, Ingrid." Matteo turned to his mother. "You're my mother but I don't know if I can forgive you." Releasing a frustrated sigh, he sat back in his chair. "Explain to me how you thought this half-baked plan would work. There are enough holes in it to drive one of our company trucks through."

Valentina licked her lips and looked at Ingrid, then back to Matteo. "We talked of it when Chloe returned, but didn't know how we'd accomplish what we wanted." She rubbed her temples. "I changed my mind and told Ingrid our plan to steal the vase was off. I couldn't go through with it. I've seen how happy Chloe makes you. I didn't want you hurt."

Valentina turned accusing eyes to Ingrid. "Is this why you insisted we go to Ravello early this morning? So, we'd miss the police?"

Ingrid shrugged.

Matteo focused his attention on the Swede. "You stole the vase on your own? And just how did you plan to frame Chloe for the theft?"

Ingrid shifted in her chair, her face twisted with discomfort. "When we heard she was leaving, I figured out what I needed to do. I stole the vase early this morning and waited until she left her room to visit Giuseppe. Her packed suitcases were by her bedroom door. I hid the Murano in her suitcase and left as Nunzio was coming for the luggage. He didn't see me. If the vase was in her suitcase, it would show when the luggage was scanned. The authorities would get suspicious about her leaving with such a valuable piece. They'd learn it was stolen and arrest her."

"You clearly didn't think your plan out," Matteo said. "The airport authorities might have assumed the vase was a souvenir Chloe was taking home, and the news of the theft may not have reached them." He lifted an eyebrow at Ingrid.

Her face reddened. "It was all I could come up with."

Matteo slid his gaze between the women. "And neither of you considered I might love my wife and defend her? That I would never believe Chloe would steal?"

"I'm sorry, son. Forgive me."

The hurt and contrition in his mother's eyes touched his heart through his frustration and anger. No matter what she'd done, or planned to do, she was his mother. "Mama, you can't separate us. Chloe and I love each other and will raise our children together."

She blinked. "Children?"

"I've just learned she and I have twins."

"I have grandchildren? Please let me see them. I promise I will treat Chloe better. I am disappointed you married an American, but she makes you happy." She rubbed her eyes and leaned closer. "Although it is hard, I have tried lately to be nicer to Chloe, to accept her into the family. I want to be a good grandmother to my grandchildren. Please give me another chance."

"We will see. You still had a hand in stealing the vase, even if you changed your mind. How did you get the security code and the keys?"

Valentina's face reddened. "I told Francesca I was

bringing some friends for a private tour and needed the code."

"And the keys?" he asked.

"I went into Francesca's office one day when she was tied up with customers. I searched her desk until I found her extra keys."

"You thought you were very clever, didn't you?" He turned to Ingrid. "You really believed I'd marry you if Chloe were out of my life?"

She looked down and back up to him. "You loved me once. I hoped you could again." Her eyes flashed with fear. "I am all alone with no one to take care of me. Please understand."

He pushed up from his chair. "I'm not interested in anything you have to offer, Ingrid. You're lucky we recovered the vase. We persuaded the police the theft was a family matter. You won't go to prison, but I want you out of here today."

She sobbed. "Please, no. I can't go back to that small apartment. I have no money. Help me."

Matteo didn't want to feel the pity that coursed through him. Ingrid tried to hurt the woman he loved. For that, he could never forgive her. But the fearful woman before him was pathetic and someone to feel sorry for.

"You're a smart woman, Ingrid," he said softly. "A talented artist with a degree, who speaks several languages. Maybe the Swedish embassy in Rome can help you find a job, but you have to leave here now."

CHAPTER 26

Caught between sleep and wakefulness, Chloe enjoyed her semi-dream state, relaxed and languorous. The memory of the past twenty-four hours thrust into her tranquility and she opened her eyes fully.

Yesterday, Matteo ordered Ingrid to move out of the villa and back to her apartment in Ravello. A chastened Valentina would continue to live at the villa. Neither Matteo nor Giuseppe were cruel, and Chloe knew they'd forgive Valentina. Maybe she and Matteo's mother would one day grow to like each other. Valentina was the twins' grandmother, and Chloe wouldn't keep her from them.

Late last night, Chloe called Justin and explained she and Matteo had reconciled. She hated hurting him. He was a good man who deserved a woman who loved him with all her heart. She hoped he found that woman.

A light rap on the door made her look over. Matteo, carrying a tray with two plates, a carafe, and cups entered the room.

"Good morning, cara mia. I've brought breakfast."

"I'm hungry." Her face heated. "I worked up an appetite after what we did in bed last night."

He laughed softly. "I hope to help you work up an appetite every night." He set the tray down on the sitting room table. "Come eat. But first, I have something for you."

"That sounds intriguing." She yawned, then threw off her covers and climbed out of bed. "What do you have?" she asked, approaching him.

He reached into his pocket and withdrew a small jewel box. Taking her hand, he knelt in front of her and opened the box to reveal a diamond ring, the large round stone surrounded by smaller ones. Her engagement ring.

Tears moistened her eyes.

"Chloe DiMarco, be my wife forever." He took the ring out of its box and slipped it onto her finger.

She held out her hand. Sunlight touched the stone, sending iridescent sparks reflecting on the walls. "My engagement ring. Thank you, Matteo. Yes, I'm your wife now and forever."

He took her into his arms and kissed her, a fervent kiss that told her how much he loved her. Finally, he held her away from him. "The ring was yours to keep. Why did you leave it?"

"It belonged to your grandmother. I couldn't take it."

"It's yours now, and later little Sofia's."

"God, I love you." She placed her hands on his shoulders and rose up to kiss his enticing lips.

He grinned. "Let's have breakfast."

Ravenous, Chloe ate quickly, not stopping to talk. Matteo watched her with an amused expression.

Finally full, she poured herself another cup of coffee and relaxed into her chair.

"Are you finished?" he asked, laughter in his voice. "Do you want another breakfast?"

"No, I'm full, for now. So much happened yesterday, I didn't eat much."

He stood, took her cup from her, and helped her stand. "Ready to work up another appetite?"

"Yes, please."

AFTERWARDS, they snuggled together in the bed. Chloe sighed with contentment and sexual satisfaction. Hope soared for their future. She and Matteo would face any obstacles together, a family, a united front.

He shifted to a sitting position and took her with him. She rested her head on his chest. The steady beat of his heart comforted her.

"I thought I'd lost you again." He kissed the top of her head.

She pressed closer and looked up into his eyes. "I thought you hated me because of what I did with the children. I hoped if we had some time away from each other, we'd resolve our differences. I realized I was wrong, that running never solved anything. I couldn't do it a second time."

"Whatever problems we have in the future, we'll solve them together."

Chloe moved away from him and sat straighter. "That was selfish of me to keep the twins from you."

"We won't speak of that. It's over. I want our marriage to last. I'm sorry I expected you to do whatever I wanted, to believe whatever I told you. I didn't respect you or your needs. I never want that to happen again. I should have followed you to Philadelphia, should have realized what those women and others did to you."

"We both made mistakes. No more 'shoulds,' only trust from now on."

He smoothed hair back from her face. "I was a stubborn jerk who didn't appreciate what you were going through. When I figured Mama and Ingrid had set you up for the theft of the vase, it all became clearer. I understand why you were afraid for the children."

She put her finger to his lips. "We've learned and we've moved on. We'll be a family now, a real family."

"You and the children are my life. Tell me about them."

"They're smart. They have a good vocabulary for their age. When they're older, I want them to learn Italian. That's why I've been studying it." She told him all she could about the twins, her joys and love.

"Thank you," he said when she'd finished. "I love them already."

"And I love you."

She raised her face for his kiss, one filled with passion, understanding, promise. And love.

CHAPTER 27

The plane began its descent into the small airport in Northeast Philadelphia. Chloe sat at a window seat. Smog blanketed the city. As much as she loved Ravello, Philadelphia would always be part of her.

Giuseppe accompanied them, but still reeling over Valentina's part in planning the theft of the vase, they refused her tearful pleas to take her also. Not having the heart to deny her the grandchildren, Chloe and Matteo promised she would meet them when they came to Italy.

Despite the private sleeping quarters on the jet, anxiety kept Chloe from a deep sleep. Tired now, adrenaline and lots of coffee gave her energy.

"Happy to see the children?" Matteo, seated next to her, asked.

She turned to him with a smile and clutched his hand. "Oh, yes, I've missed them so much."

"They're lucky to have you for a mother." He placed a loving kiss on her lips.

"It does my heart good to see you both so happy," Giuseppe remarked from his seat across the aisle.

"You'd better take care of your heart, Grandfather," Matteo said. "No more scaring us."

A smug look on his face, Giuseppe chuckled. "My plan worked. And I'm a good actor."

"Yes, but from now on, total honesty. Deal?" Chloe said.

"Deal."

Any doubts she had lifted like the smog dissolving from the Philadelphia sky. Last night, after hours of blissful pleasure, she and Matteo discussed their future. They would live between Philadelphia and Ravello. When in Philadelphia, Chloe would run her gallery and Matteo would do whatever work he could from that city. Chloe agreed to take on a partner who could handle her business when she was in Italy. They would make adjustments as needed.

She leaned against her husband's shoulder and rubbed the silver pendant at her neck. So much had happened since the day she bought the pendant, the day she met Matteo. They were in this life together, forever.

The plane taxied to a smooth stop. When the fasten seat belt light went out, Chloe stood and smoothed hands down the sides of her jeans. This morning, she wore her best pair of skinny jeans with a beige silk top and beige espadrilles. Nervousness roiled her stomach.

Matteo, standing next to her, stiffened. His clenched jaw communicated his anxiety at meeting his children. She grabbed his hand and squeezed. He looked down at her with a smile that brought a lump to her throat.

They alighted from the plane, Giuseppe first. The trio made their way across the tarmac to the small waiting area. Through the large windows, Chloe saw her grinning parents. The twins jumped up and down beside them.

Chloe broke into a run. The automatic doors opened, and the twins ran to her, squealing. She dropped to one knee and embraced them, inhaling their fresh baby scents.

"Mommy! Mommy!" they screamed in unison.

She hugged them close until they squirmed. Laughing, she released them and stood. Holding their hands, she turned to Matteo.

"Joey, Sofie, this is your daddy."

The twins decided to be shy for the first time in their lives. Joey buried his head into the side of her leg, and Sofie sucked her thumb and looked up at Matteo.

Matteo got down on one knee. "Joey and Sofie, you don't know me yet, but I already love you and I'm happy to meet you."

"Daddy?" Sofie hesitated, then flung herself into Matteo's arms.

He held her close as tears spilled down his face.

Joey peeked at his twin and his father. Smiling, he too, went into Matteo's arms.

Too filled with emotion to speak, Chloe embraced her parents. Their eyes damp, they turned to Giuseppe.

"So good to see you again." Chloe's mom hugged him.

Her dad smiled at Giuseppe and held out his hand. "I'm happy you made the trip here." His smile got broader. "Glad to know you're okay, too."

Giuseppe looked down at the twins. "I'd like to meet my great-grandchildren."

Chloe swept her hand toward Giuseppe. "Children, meet your great-grandfather."

Matteo released the twins and stood.

The children looked up at Giuseppe, suddenly shy again.

"Why don't you call me grandfather," he said.

Joey frowned. "Gandfather."

Giuseppe grinned. "Close enough. Come, give me a hug."

The elderly man bent as best as he could and wrapped his arms around the twins.

"Shall we go?" Chloe's mom asked. "We hired a car and driver."

Chloe took Joey's hand as Matteo held Sofie's.

"Let's take our family home." Love gleamed from Matteo's eyes.

Heart bursting with happiness, Chloe headed home with her family, grateful to the Ravello marriage bargain that brought her life full circle.

THE END

*THANK you for reading *Ravello Marriage Bargain**

PLEASE TURN the page for Chapter One of *Ghosts of Deveraux Manor*, Chloe's friend, Charli Deveraux's story.

EXCERPT: GHOSTS OF DEVERAUX MANOR

Charlotte Deveraux dragged her heavy suitcase from the trunk of the taxi. Fumes from the exhaust pipe made her cough. The calendar said June, but her breath visible in the cool, rain-soaked air, said November. She muttered a string of curses at the driver who refused to step out of the vehicle and help. Lightning illuminated the French countryside, followed by the loud crack of thunder. Startled, she dropped to the muddy ground. Her suitcase landed on top of her.

Welcome to Normandy!

Her friend Shannon Kosta, in the act of hoisting out her own bag, slipped in the mud and tripped over her. Shannon's backside hit the ground with a thump.

The women struggled to their feet. The cab sped off, its tires kicking up watery sludge, and the open trunk jiggling.

Shannon swept wet hair away from her face. "Wow, Charli, talk about rude."

"He acted like he'd seen a ghost." Charli ran a hand

down her muddied jacket, only spreading the dirt. "We should be glad we found anyone to take us out here. As soon as we said we were going to Devereaux Manor, no one would drive us."

"What was that about? We paid that cabbie a small fortune and he left us in the dust, or muck in this case."

"My new pants are ruined. I tried to look stylish for this trip." Charli glanced around. "This sure isn't the France I pictured."

"Me, either. My jacket is ruined, too."

Charli fought tears, brought on by jet lag, sleep-deprivation, and frustration. Things had gone from bad to worse since their red-eye from Philadelphia landed in Paris early that morning.

Shannon scanned Charli and laughed. "You've got mud on your face."

"You're not looking so good yourself. Why are we standing here? Let's get the hell out of this rain and into the house. Once we dry off and have some hot tea, we'll both feel better."

"I need something stronger than tea."

"Let's go." Charli hitched her purse over her shoulder and grabbed the handle of her suitcase. She raised her gaze to Deveraux Manor, her inheritance, rising like a ghostly vision through the rain and mist. A long spruce-lined driveway led to the house. Shivering with cold and anxiety, Charli headed up the cobblestone drive, hauling her bag behind her. Shannon, pulling her own bag, followed.

The wheels of their luggage bumped over the uneven pavement. A warning of worse to come? Charli shook her head. No sleep, the long train trip from Paris to Rouen in

Normandy, the jarring taxi drive to the house, and the never-ending rain had her imagination going berserk.

"Does it ever stop raining?" Shannon shouted. "Doesn't Mother Nature know it's June?" Another flash of lightning, followed by a crash of thunder close by made Shannon scream.

The imposing house loomed out of the cloud-filled night sky, waiting for them. Three stories high, the house had a hip roof, with three dormers on the third floor and a tower with a smaller tower, or turret, on the right, its round roof rising above the house. Lightning lit the stone tower, illuminating the narrow windows circling the turret room above it. Granite stones blended with the rain, depressing and ominous. The place would fit perfectly on the cover of a Gothic romance. Charli half expected to find a brooding, dangerous hero waiting inside.

"Thank God. An overhang." Charli sighed with relief when they reached the house. The women dragged their belongings up the steep steps, puffing with the effort. At the top, Charli leaned against the wooden door, grateful for the canopy that gave respite from the downpour. They set their suitcases against the black iron railing.

"Where's the key?" Shannon hopped from foot-to-foot. "I have to dry off and pee, not in that order. I hope the plumbing works."

Charli slid her purse off her shoulder and reached into it for the ring holding the keys the lawyer sent her. He handled the estate of Jeanne Deveraux, a distant relative Charli only discovered when she learned she'd inherited the house. She snatched the keys and held them up. "Here they are."

Gripping the large iron key, she struggled to find the keyhole in the dark. A strong gust of wind whipped through, ripping the keys from her hand. “What the…?”

“What happened?” Shannon asked.

Choking back panic, Charli scanned the steps and around the landing. “The keys are gone.”

ABOUT THE AUTHOR

An award-winning and eclectic author, Cara Marsi is published in romantic suspense, paranormal romance, and contemporary romance. She loves a good love story, and believes that everyone deserves a second chance at love. Sexy, sweet, thrilling, or magical, Cara's stories are first and foremost about the love. Treat yourself today, with a taste of romance.

When not traveling or dreaming of traveling, Cara and her husband live on the East Coast of the United States in a house ruled by two spoiled cats who compete for attention.

Connect with Cara at:

www.facebook.com/authorcaramarsi

www.pinterest.com/caramarsi/

www.instagram.com/carolyn2829

https://www.bookbub.com/authors/cara-marsi

Sign up for her newsletter and read about all her books at www.caramarsi.com

BOOKS BY CARA MARSI

A Catered Romance

A Cat's Tale & Other Love Stories

(All stories in this anthology are available separately)

A Cinderella Christmas

A Groom for Christmas (Love On a Dare Book 1)

Wedded On a Dare (Love On a Dare Book 2)

Love On a Dare Duet Boxed Set

Accidental Love

Capri Nights

Curating Love (Amore Italiano Book 1)

Ravello Marriage Bargain (Amore Italiano Book 2)

Cursed Mates

Ghosts of Deveraux Manor

Her Forever Husband

Her Snow White Christmas (Snow Globe Magic Book 1)

Her Frog Prince Holiday (Snow Globe Magic Book 2)

Her Red Riding Hood Valentine (Snow Globe Magic Book 3)

Snow Globe Magic Holiday Boxed Set

Logan's Redemption (Redemption Book 1)

Franco's Fortune (Redemption Book 2)

Luke's Temptation (Redemption Book 3)

Josh's Salvation (Redemption Book 4)

The Redemption Series Boxed Set

Love Potion

Loving Or Nothing

Murder, Mi Amore

Storm of Desire

Sweet Temptations

Sweet Temptations Boxed Set

The One Who Got Away

The Ring

Wedded in Vegas (Gambling on Love Book 1)

Love by Chance (Gambling on Love Book 2)

A Very Vegas Christmas (Gambling on Love Book 3)

The Gambling on Love Trilogy

Wedding Dreams Boxed Set

MULT-AUTHOR BOXED SETS

Brandywine Brides: A Blackwood Legacy Anthology

Sizzling Summer Boxed Set

The Marriage Coin Boxed Set

Read excerpts at www.caramarsi.com

All books available at online booksellers

A Catered Romance, A Groom for Christmas, Brandywine Brides: A Blackwood Legacy Anthology, Amore Italiano Duet,

Capri Nights, Cursed Mates, Franco's Fortune, Logan's Redemption, Love On a Dare Duet, Loving Or Nothing, Luke's Temptation, Murder, Mi Amore, Snow Globe Magic, The Gambling on Love Trilogy, The Marriage Coin, and Wedded On a Dare, are available in print.

www.ingramcontent.com/pod-product-compliance
Lightning Source LLC
Chambersburg PA
CBHW072225170626
46813CB00003B/1088
9780996981149